Under Cover

By

Karen S. Meyer

DEDICATION

.

To my children, who enjoyed listening
to me read these novels aloud to them.

Table of Contents

Contents

Dedicated To

Ted Meyer, my dream weaver who never ceases to inspire me.

F

FORWARD

When I first started writing this series, my children were 13, 11, 8, 4 and 2 years old. The older two were bringing home choose your own adventure books from the school library which were showing young women as sex objects; as simple minded, non-goal oriented, females with the inability to say a sentence without the word, "like" interjected.

I wanted them to be strong. I wanted them to be able to take anything that was dealt to them harshly in this life and turn it into something easy yet amazing. In short, I was having a difficult time finding strong stories about courageous people other than some of the stalwarts we grew up with. I decided to show them that I could create someone who was strong, smart, accomplished and could have the world as her oyster. Andie Atkins is the oldest daughter of a large family. She indeed has all the makings of my heroine and then some. She isn't used to being teased. She feels as the oldest in her family, she has that privilege, so when she meets her match at the Academy at

Quantico, she sets out to beat him at every level of competition.

Enter Anson Wellings, the grandson of General Douglas MacArthur, who finishes his Naval and Academy days with an approved pseudo name of Anson Wellings to avoid any undue attention or harassment. At least, that is his cover story. His father is the former Ambassador to Mexico where Anson grew up as an only child. He has lived most of his life with a chip on his shoulder daring others to contend with him. Now he is suffering from Post Traumatic Stress Syndrome from a crash in the Top Gun program.

A more unlikely pair never fell for each other like these two did when the Director, on Graduation Day gave them the opportunity of a lifetime to serve their country....together. Should these two, who are not fans of each other's antics, decide to take this challenge, the Director of the FBI feels they could infiltrate the spy ring of Russians if they would pose as a young newlywed couple. He adds an unusual twist. He states the Russians would never suspect them if they were embedded into the Latter-day Saint culture. He fills the library of their rented mansion with scriptures, literature and uplifting books about living a life of honesty centered around the teachings of Jesus Christ. His advice to them? "…read it, learn it, live it!"

The story centers around a real life espionage scenario that occurred in the Conejo Valley in 1989-1990 at the Northrop plant. It was suspected that plans were being stolen from the Thousand Oaks facility. In this novel, because I use some evidence received from a neighbor of mine who was employed there, which would be construed as hearsay, we deal with some ideas of how it actually could have happened. In 1989, protected secrets of government contracts, especially for the coveted B2 stealth bomber were in their infancy and not all means of protection had been explored. For this reason, I refer to the plant as Northrop instead of Northrup-Grummond, and/or Rockwell Aerospace. Here are a few of the headlines which left homes abandoned as people were laid off their jobs at that time. Three of them were our neighbors who had ideas how and why their lives were changed forever.

1. www.latimes.com ›   archives   ›   la-xpm-1990/05/15-me**Northrop to Cut More Newbury Park Jobs : Defense ...**

May 15, 1990 · May 15, 1990 12 AM PT. TIMES STAFF WRITER. Northrop Corp., a major Ventura County employer stung by drastic cuts in federal defense spending, is laying off about 6% percent of its 2,000-employee...

2. **www.latimes.com** › archives › la-xpm-1989/05/18-fi**Northrop to Cut Up to 3,000 Jobs by End of Year**

May 18, 1989 · Northrop will cut its work force by 2,500 to 3,000 by year's end, reflecting an effort to trim overhead expenses throughout the company and to reduce jobs in the massive B-2 stealth bomber...

3. **www.airfields-freeman.com** › CA › Airfields_CA_Ventura**Abandoned & Little-Known Airfields: California - Ventura area**

Sep 19, 2019 · According to Jeanette Berard of the Thousand Oaks Library, "In the 5/4/89 Conejo News, Janss Investments announced plans to build the new Rancho Conejo Airport and to abandon the older airstrip ,[the Conejo Valley Airport], and move the hangars as soon as the new strip was finished."

4. **www.upi.com** › Archives › 1989/06/06**Northrop to close Anaheim facility - UPI Archives**

Jun 6, 1989 · June 6, 1989. Northrop to close Anaheim facility. By DAVE McNARY, UPI Business Writer. LOS ANGELES -- Defense contractor Northrop Corp., in another cutback in operations,

Many of the things you read may sound strange because they will immerse themselves in the culture of the people who are members of the Church of Jesus Christ of

Latter Day Saints. Some of the funnier things come from misunderstanding their particular language. I write about them because many of those things actually happened to me. Yes, we went to Happy Steak when the people told us as new members, that we were meeting at the Stake House. Yes, we waited for three hours looking for a familiar face. , Two completely different things!

I hope you enjoy this fast paced series full of adventure, mystery, intrigue, strong female and male characters and of course, no profanity. Thank you for leaving a kind review!

Karen S. Meyer

1 Graduation Day

Graduation day at the Federal Bureau of Investigation was usually an exciting day for any graduate of the Academy. There was one new agent, however, who was beside herself with nervous anxiety.

Andrea Atkins, or as the agents called her, Andie, had been chosen as the Valedictorian of the class of 1989. She looked back at her time there at the Academy with mixed emotions. She had to work harder than any other recruit, and yes, any other woman, to prove herself worthy of the title of Agent.

There were times when she wanted to throw in the towel and give up, but she never let anyone know it. The men were hard on her, but she knew they had to be. Other agents couldn't take a chance on becoming a partner with someone who could not take the pressure and responsibility of the job. Women, stereotypically, were viewed as weaker, gentler, more emotional and the worse feared by all men, unpredictable. It was what some would say, a sexist comment, but it was how a lot of men felt through the sixties to the nineties.

There were precious little moments when she could shed tears of emotional upheaval and now she could finally let down in the solitude of her room. She had just finished her speech to the Graduating Class. She had made it, but her roommate could not handle the pressure. Sandy had dropped out leaving Andie to fight the high male population alone. *I made it! Not only that, I beat out Steve Jennings and Anson Wellings in almost every category,* she mused. Relief felt good.

She could hardly stand the sight of them. They had teased her every day of her stay there, chiding biting words like:

"Oh macho woman – thinks she can beat us at everything!"

That was nothing. The little practical jokes they played on her were almost more than she could stand, but stand them she did. For instance, once, they snuck into the locker room and filled her locker with GI Joe dolls with a note saying, "Here' you'd better practice on these guys – they are about your speed." She wasn't sure which of the two genius' was the mastermind, but she had her suspicions.

Andie was not really sure where her power came from but that was the day that she got her hips in on Anson Wellings and threw him down on the mat. They hadn't spoken since that day, and strangely enough, the practical jokes stopped. She gained a new respect in his eyes and he made sure that Steve stopped too.

He had never apologized. Anson was a little too smug for apologies, but sometimes, he would show it in other ways. It wasn't that he didn't like her but he just didn't want anything to do with working with a woman. She was pretty enough, but pretty didn't have anything to do with ability. It had everything to do with distraction. He had been raised with the words ingrained in his psyche, "…that men go out and protect the community,". It was an archaic notion in this day and age but none the less, he could not honestly condone a woman working alongside another man in a dangerous situation. He would soon learn that his family did him a grave injustice by instilling ideas of inequality between the sexes.

Now, after graduation, waiting in the Director's office for his assignment, Anson wondered what brave new world awaited and where his presence would be required. He sat nervously as the door opened to the outer office.

Andie calmly took her place in the waiting area, glancing up only to meet Anson's eyes. "Great," she huffed under her breath, "What's HE doing here?"

The Director's secretary picked up the phone, nodded, and then addressed the two. "You both may go in now. The Director is ready to see you," she smiled.

BOTH? What is this? Confusion was written on both their faces. It was highly unusual for two agents to meet with the Director at the same time unless disciplinary measures were to be taken.

"Andie. Anson. Come in and sit down. I'll get right to the point. I am sure you are both wondering why your assignments were not posted on the board like everyone else's," he began.

The thought had crossed my mind, Anson nodded and tried to appear aloof.

I was SURE I hadn't flunked, Andie smiled knowingly.

"The reason you are here is because you have been selected for a special mission on the West Coast. This is over my head, actually. It appears that the Reds have a line on every agent that is presently operating on the Coast and we need some new blood." He got up and went over to the window.

"I don't like to throw my best Agents to the wolves like this, but after seeing what you have been able to accomplish, you're the only two who are qualified for the job." He turned and with pipe in hand, sat on the corner of the desk facing Anson.

"Anson you are not as young as most of the Agents graduating today. Quite frankly, you have more experience than most of them in combatants and aeronautical fields. I wish we had more of you Top Gun graduates applying here. This job will rely heavily on your knowledge that you have received at Officer Training in

Annapolis, combined with your degree in Criminal Law and the practical experience you have received here at the Academy. The fact that some of your training was also in France is just gravy. You do still speak some French, don't you?" he queried.

"Oui, mon Capitan, un poi," Anson shook his hand motioning, "a little".

"Great. I am sure you can get by with that. Now, Andie," he said turning to her and smiling.

Returning the smile, she tipped her head to the side, wondering just what it was that made her such an attractive applicant for a dangerous mission. *It is dangerous, isn't it? I didn't get into this just to babysit the likes of him...,"* she smiled and nodded eagerly.

"Your grades were tops. You had to try harder than any woman we have ever had here. I am sorry that the guys didn't make it any easier," he sneered a side look at Anson. "It's a jungle out there and you have to be prepared for the worst. I have no doubt that you can do any task that is presented to you. The hard part will be convincing your partner that you are up to snuff. I am afraid that I know who played most of the shenanigans on you during your term here...," with one eyebrow raised, he stole a glance in Anson's direction.

Anson slumped an inch in his chair and Andie shot a glance of venom towards him, then defiantly, she spoke out of turn to the Director.

"You knew…and didn't…!" realizing her place, she stopped and looked downward to recapture her composure.

"Yes, darn it. I knew and if I had bailed you out of it, you'd not have the strength of character that you have now. You are not just a woman, you 're a woman with a license to kill. I had to know that you could take it out there! I'd do it again," he said tersely, then relaxed and smiled.

"For what it's worth, sir, I'm sorry that I took part in those pranks," said Anson, who was obviously brown nosing the Director.

"Save it, Wellings. You've got to prove it to HER now. You two are going to be partners on this operation. You've got to learn to trust each other implicitly. After it's over, the head of operations on the West Coast has generously allowed you to have the option of choosing your home base and a generous bonus, which is a luxury *never* afforded a Rookie, I dare say."

That's it. I risk two years of my life flying wingman to Bruiser, the most insane pilot who ever held a throttle and now I've got a partner whose finger is going to freeze on the trigger when she breaks a nail. That is how I am going to die. It's not going to be a pretty sight. Anson stretched back in his chair and took a deep breath.

The Director touched some papers on his desk as he sat down. "You will pose as an Aeronautical Engineer for

Northrup, transferred here from their Louisiana facility to work specifically on the Top Secret cloaking system of the new B2 bomber. The Russians want this and they are willing to kill to get it so be on your toes. With this device decoded, they can detect any one of our planes when they take off and know where they are going. Without it, we carry the upper hand," he smirked.

"But sir, I was just a throttle jockey in the Navy, nothing more. I certainly do not have a PhD in Aeronautical Engineering. How can I carry this off?" he wondered out loud.

"Don't be so modest, Wellings. I saw your jacket when you put into our port. The job you did on those Libyan air pirates was not too shabby. That is something to be proud of. Being top secret, of course, it wasn't published in the newspaper as to who made the direct hits, who performed reconnaissance and got us the vital information that saved the hostages, but don't think for a minute you were overlooked. No, you have more experience with planes than any of our new guys and your grades were almost as good as Atkins here in espionage, weaponry and tactical diversions. You were perfect for the job," he puffed away on his pipe proudly.

Andie smiled as Anson cringed. *Her again.*

"Sir, where exactly do I fit in?" she wondered aloud.

"I'm getting to that. Northrup has a dynamite security system. They know that John Smithe in Contracts and

Negotiations is probably the leak, but they can't seem to catch him with any evidence to pin anything on him. He comes up clean every time there is a briefcase check, but the projects that he has access to usually wind up on our list of things that our double agents say the Russians have recently acquired in their intelligence. To keep it going, Northrup has been giving John things to work on that say Top Secret, but really are nothing new," he shook his head at the very thought of someone committing the act of treason.

"Ok, so you want me to befriend this guy and find out what makes him tick?" Anson was hungry for more information.

"Oh, we know what makes him tick. He's in love with a wife who has a cocaine or some kind of habit. She needs drugs and his Northrup salary and schedule of benefits clearly does not allow for cocaine. It looks like he's been getting just enough from the Reds to keep her satisfied, but we think he wants enough money to put her through a rehabilitation therapy program. There might be more to that story than we are seeing. He's going for the big bucks so he can get out of this for good, or so he thinks. He'll have to do some time for being a naughty boy."

"Does his wife know what he is doing?" Andie asked.

"That's where you come in, Andie. You and Anson are going to be the perfect Mormon newlyweds. Hubby and wife. You are going to become their dearest friends as their new neighbors. You know, carpool to work, bar-b-ques, shopping, doing lunch. I want you to bug every room of that house. I don't think the wife knows anything, but John's contact, we think is the infamous Ivan Doblinsky of the KGB. That's right, the one you heard of in your classes. No one has ever seen him and he hates Mormons because they are so darned honest and can't usually be swayed to the dark side," the Detective began to unfold the story.

"But Director, there are lots of FBI Agents that are Mormon. Won't they suspect?" Anson inquired.

"Anson, they suspect everyone and anyone, but they won't expect the FBI to do something as stupid as to put a man and wife team who happen to be Mormon and work at Northrup right across the street from a suspected subversive. They clearly won't suspect the obvious," he said proudly.

Andie piped up, "Ingenious Director! My compliments," Andie said.

"Precisely why you were chosen for this job, Andie. You think like a spy and your Russian language grades were tops! I like that!" he winked.

"Why, thankyou sir. I'm glad *someone* appreciates me around here," she dared not do such a familiar thing as to wink back.

Suddenly the Director glanced over and saw that Anson was squirming around in his chair.

"I'll say this one time, and one time only. You two are going to have to act like you like each other. No, like you love each other. By the looks on your faces, it's going to be the toughest undercover job you will probably never have to do. But…I expect you to do it and do it well. I'll not be embarrassed by your lack of professionalism. Understood?" He clearly wanted to know.

They nodded in response and forced a smile to each other.

"Now here are your plane tickets. Your contact will be wearing a Century 21 Jacket at the terminal annex at LAX. Your "Real Estate Agent," Jack Gibbens will take you to your new love nest, which movers are putting the finishing touch on everything…," he laughed, looking at his watch. We've also included a whole library on Mormon Literature so you will have the Church History program to bone up on. But, you will find all that in your den when you get there.

"We'll let you do your own personal unpacking in your separate bedrooms, but the rest of the house has been completely decorated and furnished by the Bureau. For looks only, we have created a Master Bedroom, but the place is huge! Not only will you have our own rooms, but directly facing their house across the street on the second floor, we will have a complete surveillance team room for you. Everything – state of the art, trust me."

"Andie, here is a list of your contacts: Hairdresser, Interior Decorator, and we've hired you a housekeeper and handyman. They really are married and have both been in active and active for the bureau for about 30 years. They will live in the guest house out back and do surveillance whenever you can't."

"I've always wanted a maid," she smiled wistfully.

"Don't get too excited. Don't be ordering her around as she is just there to assist. It's just that it wouldn't do for you to be vacuuming when Ivan called or walked up to the front door, now would it? They are there, seriously, as back up. They are both very capable," he was intent on that.

"Okay, Director. I've done a lot of studying before, but how do I cram for becoming a Mormon? I mean, won't the church members know that I don't know anything?"

"What about you Andie, do you have any experience with this religion?" he asked, half expecting her to be one of those true-blue-dyed-in-the-wool Mormons already.

"Well, no, but I've always prided myself on being a fast study," she laughed.

"You'll have to be. Here are a couple of books that they read on a regular basis. They use it along with the Bible and say that it is a second witness to Jesus Christ. Read it, learn it, know it, live it. Whatever your vices are, they stop today. Whether it is drinking, smoking, coffee, quit now. You'll have at least five hours to read this book on the plane. I suggest you get home and start packing. Your plane leaves Dulles at 7:00 tomorrow morning," he stated in a matter of fact manner.

"Sir, since that one crash Bruiser and I had at Top Gun, I don't like planes much anymore. Do you suppose I could have a little nip on the plane? You know, to relax me?" Anson spoke quietly.

"Read it, learn it, know it, live it, Wellings. I know about the crash, it's like riding a horse; you fall off, you get back on. Stop being such a baby. Here's your packet. You are now Mr. and Mrs. Anson and Andie Wellings," he said with finality.

"Sir, one more thing. I don't know about this Mormon thing. Won't the Russians know that I've never been on a Mission? Or what if they check Anson MacArthur for service records and find nothing? They'll know I'm a fake," Anson was clearly worried. He felt that swell of anxiety rise in his abdomen.

"Wellings, there is one thing you don't know yet about the Bureau. We think of everything. We have altered and created records. We're good at that. So good, that we will let them or anyone who wishes to know, see that you, yes, you, were the Libyan hero. We will show them that you were Mr. Annapolis and that you even went to MIT," he walked around his desk.

"We simply exchanged the Criminal Law for Aeronautical Engineering degrees, and deleted anything about the FBI. We also mentioned that you went on a Mission for your church to France when you were 19.

That's been 11 years ago. If anyone wants you to speak French, merely tell them that with the years, you simply put that ability behind you. You'll find, in the future, not to ask such mundane questions, Agent Wellings. That will be all. Good luck and enjoy your flight, Mr. and Mrs. Wellings," he spoke with finality.

He spoke with a finality which made them automatically rise and shake his hand. They departed his office quickly and stood in the lobby with blank stares at each other. What had they gotten themselves into? They spoke briefly in the lobby.

"Let me have my identification and plane ticket. I'll meet you at the airport tomorrow at 6:15," Andie spoke gruffly to her new husband.

"Just hold onto your horses. I've got the packet and I am the man of the house. Here's your identification, but I'll hold onto the plane tickets. Wow, what are these? We get cars too?" he asked holding up two sets of car keys.

"I'll ignore your chauvinist behavior for now. You're right, we may as well start traveling together. Pick me up at my apartment tomorrow. We'll share a cab. You can pay for it. Those look like our new California car keys. What type do you think are waiting for us in the garage of our new home?" she wondered.

"It says here, Ford Taurus station wagon and a Chevrolet GEO. Gee, the all American family. I was hoping for a Lamborghini. Now all we need is a couple of kids," he sneered.

"Yeah, well think of me as temporarily infertile. I've got dibs on the Taurus," she shot back.

"See? We're working together as a team already," he forced a grin. "See you at 6:15 sharp. Say, you're not one of those wives that are late all the time are you?" he teased.

"About as much as you're a couch potato. Cut the crud, Cowboy! See you tomorrow and don't forget to get rid of anything with your initials on it, handkerchiefs, stationery, luggage," she twirled around and made for the exit.

After they left, the Director came out and spoke to the secretary. "Well, Ellen, do you think they are going to make it?"

"No problem, Director. They're already talking as if they have been married for 10 years.

*   *   *

The 747 began its descent. Anson held onto the seat arm with a death grip as he read from his Book of Mormon. Andie glanced down and felt a pang of empathy for him but tried hard to cover it up.

"You ok?" she asked sympathetically.

"Yeah, it's the first dry trip I've ever made. I am doing just fine," he lied.

"Good," she teased, "the stewardess said we might have to circle for a while. It seems they've got fog..." her voice trailed off. She smiled as she watched his knuckles go white.

As they landed, they began the tedious task of recovering luggage from the huge carousel before them. Suddenly a large man grabbed for Andie's shoulder bag from behind. Feeling his presence, she instinctively elbowed him in the ribs as she stomped on his foot with her high heel. Then she took two steps out and executed a perfect roundhouse kick, scraping her high heel across his face. Next she grabbed two pieces of luggage and threw the first to his groin and the heavier one directly to his head, keeling him over onto his back – out cold.

Anson folded his arms and watched on in awe as she slapped her hands together in finality and straightened the jacket to her suit. Security guards were on the scene like flies to honey and were asking questions all at once faster than they could be answered.

"What happened, Lady?" The tall TSA guard asked.

"Who are YOU?" the other one asked Anson.

"This guy tried to grab my purse and I let him have it, that's all," she tried to explain as calmly as she could.

"Who? THIS guy?" they asked pointing at Anson.

"No, that guy down there with blood all over him. This guy is…," she hesitated.

"I'm…. her husband. And…. I'm awfully proud of her," Anson smiled and said with honesty.

And so it had begun.

2 A New World

Jack Gibbens, looked sharp donning his Century 21 gold jacket. He walked confidently up to the scene of the crime. Surveying the situation, he quickly assessed what needed to get done.

"Say! Mr. and Mrs. Wellings! Right here!" he commanded attention as the TSA detail whirled to the sound of his voice. "What's going on here, folks?" he asked innocently.

The TSA guy started to cut him off. Getting close to the couple was not what he had in mind. He needed to fill out some paperwork and didn't need some Real Estate jerk to break in on his bust.

"I'm sorry sir, but could you step back? We're trying to work here. Thank you very much," he said gently maneuvering Jack back a few inches.

Jack's voice lowered an octave as he spoke an inch or two from the lad's face. Suddenly his black ops background kicked in and quietly holding his FBI badge in hand, he remarked, "Now, let's just handle this calmly and quietly. These people are under my protection and I need to get them out of here. It's a matter of National Security, got the picture? Now, be a hero and clear the way for us and you can tell your grandchildren that you helped America," he smiled a waxy toothy grin as he slipped his badge effortlessly into his pocket.

"Alright, folks, let's break it up, we've got this under control. Mr. and Mrs. Wellings, you are free to go now. We'll take care of this perp. You have a nice day. Hope you enjoy your stay in Los Angeles," he tipped his hat and flashed a smile at Jack to see if he was doing okay.

A nod from Jack and a few minutes later as they entered the Century 21 car, Andie spoke quietly. "Okay, what was that all about? I was pretty sure we were going to be detained as witnesses to a felony and tied up with paperwork all day," she wondered out loud.

"Yeah," Anson wondered, "How did you do that? I had us pegged for at least two hours of paperwork. Thanks!"

"It's simple, my good people. You'll find in this business that your FBI badge will literally open doors. People want to help their country and they know we can do it. It's just simple. Those guys will detain that crook for a while, scare him pretty bad, and maybe trump up something victimless, like vagrancy. Then they'll let him go. He will go home with a terrific story to tell the wife and kids. Ah! America!" he laughed.

"You're taking this pretty lightly. We thought we were the only Bureau people on this case. The Director told us that the Reds knew all the agents on the West Coast," Anson wanted to know the plan.

Jack turned on his booming voice from the front seat of the car. "You're right. This is an "import" plan. Sorry, we didn't get properly introduced. Jack Gibbens is the name, Florida's same. Only there, my name is John Biggins. Just screws 'em up computer wise. I've disappeared in their eyes. My hair's different and I've got colored contacts on and a moustache. Come 'on. They told you how this goes, didn't they?" he sounded surprised.

"We were told all that we were supposed to know. You and our other contacts are supposed to tell us what we need to know, that's all," Andie spoke.

"Well, my cover is only as good as their agent's memories. If they have moved any of their operatives out here and one makes me, it's over, but that's half the game. They don't usually do this sort of thing. We brought in agents that have been retired for over 25 years or are completely new, like you. Your hairdresser, Andie, used to be a secretary at the Los Angeles Office, of course, trained as agent much earlier. They won't be looking for her.

Andie spoke frankly, "What do you mean, 'they won't be looking for her?',", she wanted to know.

"She's been out of the loop too long. Your housekeeper and handyman were agents years ago and retired. Long forgotten. Your interior decorator was a markswoman with the Secret Service but she was FBI first. Her last assignment was in Dallas, November 1963. She retired after Kennedy passed. She just couldn't take it that they let him down. We had to do a lot of talking, but we got her to take the assignment. Trust me, we know what we're doing," Jack encouraged.

"Good," Andie smiled. Where are we now? Are we close to the house?"

"We're about to turn West on the 101 freeway, Andie. We've got about a 30-minute ride before we get to your house, and believe me, it's a looker. I don't know what you guys had to do to get such a cushy first assignment. Why don't you just enjoy the scenery and I'll let you know more when we get closer."

Andie was already asleep in the back seat. Anson sat intently reading his Book of Mormon.

The hills in Westlake Village were a lovely shade of Kelly green this time of year. The house that the Wellingss were to occupy overlooked the most affluent section of the Village called Westlake Lake. A house on the island goes anywhere from $850,000 to $2,000,000 for a two bedroom built in 1960. Their house was a five bedroom, two story California adobe whose entry way was graced by a long sloping drive. This particular lot, on 1 ½ acres had a bungalow in the back for the housekeeper/handyman duo. They were busy readying the place for the new young tenants.

"I can't believe I'm dusting books and fixing up a library for someone else, Harry. I feel insignificant. When I think of all those years of training, and for what, to be a housekeeper?" she laughed incredulously.

"Bess Castle, be quiet. For all the money they are paying us, at our age, it's best to just do as we're told, keep our eyes open and mouths shut. We'll finally be able to take that trip to Fiji that we always wanted to do during the Cold War, he consoled.

"You're right. How is it that we never pulled assignments like this?" she asked.

"Listen Bess, you're getting senile. Don't you remember all those movie stars that we had to follow in the 50s? They were all black listed and McCarthy thought all of them were Commies. You can't have forgotten casing out Howard Duff and Ida Lupino, can you? Those were some glamourous times, Bess, glamourous times, indeed," he sighed as he unpacked yet another box of books.

"Yes, that's about the time we met. Remember we were told to go to the Coconut Grove and watch that new starlet. When you held me in your arms on the dance floor, I felt...such strength. Your cologne. I never forget the smell of your chest. I fell in love almost immediately, Harry Castle," she stopped dusting and stood staring off into space.

"Oh Bess, it was the same for me, too. I tried to be professional. I really tried to keep my mind on the assignment at hand, but the music and atmosphere and the stars in your eyes were more than I could handle," he spoke walking to her and taking her hand.

"We've had a good life, Harry. I love you!" she whispered.

"The best is yet to be, my love," he kissed her ever so gently. "Now, let's get cracking and get this place whipped into shape. We've got an assignment, don't we? I feel young again, Bess!" he slapped her behind as he exited the room.

3 The Team

As the threesome in the Real Estate car turned off the freeway onto Westlake Boulevard, no one would have guessed that they were FBI. A real estate car touring the Village was about as common as the mailman.

"Are we close? Wake up, Andie. We're here.," Anson nudged.

"Huh? Where? Oh, it's a lovely community. Look, there's a lake and ducks!" she laughed.

"Well, ducky, let's talk turkey," Jack spoke frankly. He pulled the car over to the side and turned around. Speaking into his two-way radio, it was clear that they had been followed by another agent from the Airport.

"Cappy, come in, over. About to give the specs and tour of the property, that's why we 've stopped, over."

"Affirmative, Beans. Will stand by. Cappy, out," the shaded figure in the blue car watched over them and protected them from afar.

Suddenly a momentary pang of anxiety flew over both Anson and Andie's faces. You could see what was going on in those minds. It was almost as if the dawn of realization had not occurred until this very minute.

Were really doing this! They mirrored each other's thoughts with just a look and then gathered their composure.

"Ok, you'd better brief us. I expect we'll be on our own from this point on," Anson spoke confidently.

"More or less. We'll be checking in on you from time to time, and you should call us if you get anything solid. Don't try to be heroes! I'm sure you remember from your classes that a dead hero is good to no one," he emphasized.

"We don't expect you to sit on your surveillance equipment 24 hours a day. It is set up to automatically go on when sensors detect activity, but let Harry and Bess explain all that to you. You've got to make best friends with the Smithes as soon as possible without arousing suspicion. That's not easy. Don't jump right into it. Look for an easy opening and make it look natural, got it?" he continued.

"We can do that. What about this Church thing? I'm sure the Director expects us to go on Sundays. Just how involved are we supposed to get?" Andie wondered aloud.

"You get as devout as you can. Invite them out. All Mormons do that. That won't be suspicious at all. We didn't buy all those books for looks, you know. Just let the Castles take over for you whenever you can't be there to monitor the equipment. Say, if you do have any questions, don't use the phone. It might be bugged, you never know. We don't want to take any chances. Just call me up and tell me that there's something wrong, like the plumbing, with the house. Now, let's go look at your little cottage, shall we?

Cappy? The beans are done, over. Here we go! Beans, out," he concluded.

"Is that guy going to be around all the time," they both said at the same time, then laughed nervously.

"He's your emergency backup. If something bad goes down, you'll see him soon enough, but he's pretty elusive."

"Why is he there? Aren't you good enough?" Andie smiled.

"Well, remember when I came in to get you at the airport? Supposing' we had a leak in the chain of command. Wouldn't it be nice if he saw someone bug our car or plant a little incendiary device under the tire? Would it be nice if he warned us?" his smile was disingenuous and condescending. "We don't take any chances. Remember, no dead heroes," he shook his head sadly.

"Sounds like you've been through that end before," Anson queried.

"Yep. It wasn't pretty. I had a partner with an itchy finger who didn't like to wait for back up. He wasn't very lucky," Jack said pulling into the driveway of a very beautiful house.

"I make enough money to afford *this*? What, are you kidding me?" Anson was excited.

"Yeah, you're going to be a pretty important honcho at Northrup. You did get briefed on that end, didn't you? I heard you were Top Gun and know the ins and outs of the airplane parts business," he spoke quickly.

"Sure. I'm all set. Just one thing. How long do I have to accomplish anything of strategic importance and value? I've got more than a week, don't I?" he started to squirm.

"Anson, it takes time to be a buddy to someone. We expect you to worm your way into his heart within about two to three months. Do you think you can do that? Now, if you need anything, you've got charge cards that have been cleared through the bureau. Just do one thing for Uncle Sam. Before you use those little pieces of gold, ask yourself if you truly think that it will help you get deeper into the lifestyle that is needed to capture the crook. Don't buy anything illegal, for Heaven's sake. Now get out and I'll give you the royal tour," he smiled.

Standing on the front porch, Jack suddenly took on the guise of a very savvy Real Estate Mogul. Pretending that the world was watching, he made a wide panoramic sweeping motion with his free arm, assuming to show the view. While pointing off into the distance as if to talk about the ocean over the mountains, he spoke quietly under his breath.

"The house directly across the street is where the Smithes live. Look, not directly at it, but look at the room above the garage. That appears to be John's study. Whenever he goes into the study, something very strange happens. Our listening devices, the ones that our Cable Television guys planted, go screwy," he led their eyes down to Andie's new rose garden with his sweeping gestures.

"Do you like roses Andie? Here's your new rose garden," then kneeling next to the soil, he spoke quietly again.

"It's almost as if he has a scrambling device that we don't have intelligence on yet. Very frustrating. Do you think that you can find out what is going on and disable it? The interesting thing is that when the scrambling device is activated, you would think that the telephone would be in use, but it never is. We need to know if the bugs are inadequate or if he is onto our surveillance already," he dropped the handful of dirt as they rose to a standing position.

"Let me show you the inside," again grand sweeping gestures towards the house. Curiosity seeker's drapes moved quietly around the neighborhood immediately surrounding the house as some wished to know more about the young yuppies taking over the occupancy.

Bess Castle opened the oak and stained glass front door to the abode then humbly bid them enter. She and her husband quickly got off to a good start with Andie and Anson. Standing in the entry way, Andie looked around. The off white carpets and skylights in the living room quickly gave a feeling of warmth and friendliness.

As Andie continued her maternal investigation, she was pleased with what she saw. Most of the house seemed to be a combination of dusty rose, desert teal and off white. Accents of dark green from the multitude of plants which dotted the furniture added a nice touch. The colors were not what she would have thought to choose on her own, but she was not exactly operating on a normal time line.

Usually, one goes to college, chooses a career and meets a mate. The fun of getting married is in getting to plan your colors together, fighting over décor and compromising on exactly what the bride wanted in the first place.

Yes, that was how it was supposed to be done, she chuckled to herself. "This is a little backwards, but somehow it feels like home," she spoke out loud.

"Backward, Mrs. Wellings? I know that this is a little out of the ordinary to decorate an entire home without any input from the client, but I did so hope you would like what I chose," said a disappointed voice from behind Andie.

"Oh! I beg your pardon! I didn't mean to insult...who are *you?*" Andie insisted. She had met Mrs. Castle, but this person was a stranger. Jack stopped talking to Anson for a moment to introduce them all.

"I'm sorry, Andie. Please meet your interior decorator, Inez Caruso of Interiors by Inez. She is also one of us, remember?" Jack asked and nodded at the same time.

"Oh, yes. I'm sorry. You startled me, that's all. Again, I just meant, I don't know where I would have started putting this all together. I don't even pay attention to what the latest colors are. I guess I haven't had much time to do that sort of thing lately," she apologized.

"Precisely why I was consulted. Since I retired from the Bureau, I've been working in this line of work. Something that interested me in MY youth. They say, well, they say that I am pretty talented, actually," she hesitated to boast.

"Pretty, good?" Jack laughed. "Inez's clientele is so packed that it was hard for us to get her to take the assignment, but she is the very best there is in both fields. I saw her working out at the range with a Beretta and those young gals are no match for her sharp eye," Jack winked.

"Inez, would you show me the rest of the house?" Andie smiled.

"Of course. This is a tri-level home. The living room and entry and Library are on the main entry floor with the kitchen, family room, laundry and bath downstairs. Upstairs, you'll find the Master bedroom, four bedrooms and two full baths. We've taken the liberty of putting the surveillance equipment in the room directly opposite of Mr. Smithe's den. Yours and Mr. Wellings's rooms are on the opposite sides of the Master Bedroom. Each has a lock that can be opened with a key.

"You should both place your FBI identification into the floor safe under the bed. Here's the combination. It wouldn't do for that to be lying around, your cover would be blown instantly. Our numbers are on the rolodex. Again, call us. The bureau will disavow any knowledge of your existence if you call them," she spoke a little harshly.

"Ok, so you are our only ties. When we want to come in out of the cold, we won't call the bureau. I'm assuming it's because our voice prints would not activate the file that has been changed for identification purposes. I must admit, it feels a little scary, Inez," said Andie.

"It's more for your protection than anything else. If someone put two and two together, they could get really creative and find out just who's team you play for. You'd be dead long before we could get to you," Jack sighed.

"Ok, anything else we need to know?" Anson was tired of all of this. *Let's get on with this*, he thought.

"Nope. Keep in touch," Jack sailed out the door.

"You might keep your piece in your purse, honey. There's no law against a girl protecting herself. You've got a license for it," Inez whispered.

"Oh, yeah. What about me? What protection will I have? Do I get to carry my weapon to work?" he asked sarcastically.

"Actually, you have a civilian's license also, and you should carry yours with you in your car or brief case. While you are at Northrup, the Security will protect you. Their Director of Security and Internal Affairs is fully briefed on your position. You have a meeting with him on Monday morning," she added as she left the front door open.

Andie went over to the door and closed it. She turned and rested against the door, looking down at her luggage which graced the entry way.

"Well, dear. Shall we unpack? I'll meet you for dinner at 5:00. I think formal would be a bit much, let's blue jean it," she stretched and started upstairs with her load. "By the way, honey, what are you cooking?" she asked sweetly.

"Wait a minute. Andie, this is serious. You can't cook? You' got to cook, Andie. All I know how to do is nuke food. You're the wife...go for it," Anson begged.

"This is the 90s honey. You are a liberated husband. I tell you what. You make dinner and I'll clean up," she compromised.

"Deal," he sighed, ascending the stairs with his own bags.

At five, the phone rang violently off the hook. Anson and Andie ran from room to room trying to locate that which they hadn't been briefed on; namely, the location of the phone!

Finally, logic and deductive reasoning gave way and they attacked it victoriously in the kitchen.

"Hello?" Anson yelled.

"Hey, buddy, you don't have to yell! Anson? Anson Wellings? Is that you?" the voice demanded an answer.

"Who is this?" Anson asked cautiously.

"Why, this is Bruiser, I mean Vaughn Adams. Do you remember me?" he laughed.

"Remember you! I spent half my Naval career trying to save your life up in those clouds, you big lug. What are you doing?" Anson was clearly happy and then realizing what just happened, froze in place with his mouth gaping in silence.

Wait.... why does Bruiser have this number. This is a private land line. The only people who have this number are the Bureau and no one else. That means, he may be the leak – the spy! He could be the Russian double agent and he is testing me right now! Thoughts were racing in Anson's mind as to what to do next. Instinct born of reality said he should remain calm, cautious and admit nothing.

Oh, I'm in trouble now. How do I safely get out of this? He KNOWS me. He knows my real name!

"Hey, I'm in the Bishopric in the Ward. When they said a young couple was moving in, they put me to work on welcoming you. The background was the same, you know, like age, Naval experience, and the first name. The thing that was throwing me for a loop was the last name. I'm sure they just made a computer error, huh? Wellings, not MacArthur!" he laughed.

"Well, actually, Bruiser, they're right," he spoke cautiously. "My Great Uncle was Douglas MacArthur. Can you imagine the heat I would have taken in the service if the guys would have known that? Not to mention the fact that anyone around me wouldn't have gotten a fair shake. You've seen how they razz other celebrity's kids. The brass knew, but that's all," he spoke confidently.

"Oh yeah! You'd have been fried! Good choice, guy!" Bruiser supported.

Anson looked Heavenward and mouthed, "Thank you God. I owe you one."

"Listen Anson. There's been a little mix up in the transfer of your records from your last ward. I know it sounds crazy, but the Salt Lake computer printout says you've never existed. What a laugh, huh? We just got a note that the records would be delayed and to contact you directly for information," he spoke nonchalantly.

Good going, FBI. Guess they couldn't get any trustworthy Mormon to falsify documents, ha ha.

"No problem. So, what's happening?" Anson had his pencil ready to copy down any news.

"Well, tomorrow night is the Blue and Gold dinner. It's at the Stake house at 7:00 pm. Why don't you join us? I'll look for you in the parking lot. Church meets at 9:00 on Sunday. That's about all for this week," he concluded.

"Okay! We'll see you there. Can't wait for you to meet the little wife. See you!" as Anson started to hang up, he heard Bruiser's voice trail off in the distance, "So what was your previous ward? What was the City and State?" and Anson's eyes got as big as saucers. Without answering he hung up without saying a word, knowing the next time he saw Bruiser, he had better have the information and it had better match this so called record that was being mailed to the local Church building.

"Okay, hot shot. What do we do first?" she asked.

"We're to meet at that Steak House, Sizzler, probably. They are having a big dinner there at 7:00 pm on Friday night. We have to wear blue and gold. Can we swing that?" he wondered out loud.

"I don't have a thing to wear! I'll have to get us something tomorrow, so give me the "plastic"! What's for dinner, I'm starving!" she asked licking her lips.

"There's nothing in the refrigerator. We're going to McDonalds! You go to the store tomorrow and get us some grub," Anson mouthed.

"Okay," she nodded in agreement.

As she pondered which set of car keys they were going to try out first, she thought about the request for them to wear certain colors. *What a weird church, why blue and gold? I look terrible in those colors!*

4 The "Steak" Out

As the Sun began to drop behind the mountains, the steel grey Ford Taurus made its final circle in the parking lot of Sizzler's Steak house. They had tried every one within a 25-mile radius. First Agoura, then Thousand Oaks, Camarillo and now had come back to the Thousand Oaks restaurant for one last pass.

"I can't understand it. I wrote it down very carefully. How could I have gotten it wrong? he spoke with his voice full of question.

"Well, actually, I'm glad. I'm going to take this awful jumpsuit back. I look just terrible in this shade of gold. That blue fly-boy suit looks pretty good on you though, why don't you keep it? You can wear it to fix the car or something. Just lose the gold scarf. Let's go home," Andie spoke wearily.

"Yeah, we've still got a lot of studying to do before Sunday. I don't want to mess up anymore," Anson spoke with determination to succeed.

"Okay, but this time, can we look up the address in the phone book? I want to get to the right Church building, ok? I mean whoever heard of a church dinner at a Steak house anyway?" she begged.

"No problem. You be in charge of getting us to Church by 9:00," Anson conceded, giving her the control that she desired.

Saturday morning, Anson cooked a huge breakfast, pancakes, eggs, bacon, juice and melon graced the table when Andie made her appearance.

"Anson, this looks like enough for an army. How are we going to eat all of this?" she asked.

"I'm sorry. I got a little carried away. I'll go ask the Castle's if they want to join us. I need them to get a message to the Bureau to make sure I know the City and State that my last church meeting house was at. I don't know if Bruiser said we were getting an award or if he needed a ward name, or something like that. When you are from a family of nine, you get used to helping to prepare this much. It just seemed natural. Let's just have the pancakes and eggs now and we'll make bacon, lettuce and tomato sandwiches and melon for lunch," he suggested.

"Okay. Thank you. I'll do the same for you another day...I'm really good at instant oatmeal. It's one of my specialties," she smiled.

The rest of the day, they spent quizzing each other on Church History and boning up on anything that they might be asked the next day.

Again, the phone rang. It was Bruiser.

"I never saw you guys last night. I have to apologize. You know, I was so excited about talking to you, I completely forgot to tell you the address of our Stake Building. Ordinarily, we would meet at the Chapel on La Venta, but sometimes we join with other Wards and have an activity. You guys don't even have a Cub Scout. I just thought you'd like to come and meet everyone. Our Stake Building is in the town of Newbury Park at the corner of Wendy and Kimber," he continued.

"Well, big guy, no problem. Next time I'll know! Yeah, those little guys DO look good in blue and gold, don't they? Listen, we'll see you bright and early tomorrow morning," Anson put Bruiser at ease.

When he hung up the phone, he stared at it for a moment and smiled at what a close call that was. Andie looked at him with a puzzled look.

"What was all that about Cub Scouts?" she queried.

"Well, he just gave me the wrong information and was clarifying where we should go. You knew that Cub Scouts wear blue and gold right?" he conned her trying desperately to save face.

"Uh, huh. We've got to try harder to go directly to the source when we have a problem. You know that book that we've been reading? Why do you think they call it the Triple combination?" she asked with that know it all look on her face.

"Because you need to unlock the knowledge with a combination lock?" he chided wondering why they called it that as well.

"No stupid. Look in the back. You can look up the answer to any problem we have in any one of the three indexes. For instance, I want to know what to wear tomorrow. So I simply go to any one of three places; the Bible Dictionary, the Joseph Smith translation or the Topical Index and it should tell me. See? Under "DRESS," it says Apparel, clothing, modesty. I am confident that when I look farther, they will say that...," she was interrupted.

"Andie, stow it. Just get up in the morning and slap on a suit and get in the car. Bring those books with you and we'll be all set," Anson insisted.

The next morning, sitting in front of the Church, Andie and Anson watched several happy families going into the building.

Suddenly Andie's head was peering back and forth as if she were watching a tennis tournament. Anson, being curious, started to move from side to side to see if he could get a better look at that which she was casing.

"What are we doing?" he asked, moving perfectly in sync with her from left to right.

"That does it. That makes fifty-three females who are wearing dresses and not one of them is wearing pants. I'm not going in there wearing this lovely grey linen pant suit, they'll know I'm not a real Mormon. Quick, "dear," in the trunk is some dry cleaning I had done yesterday. Hand me that black skirt," she pleaded.

"Okay, but you really should have taken your own advice," he laughed handing her the skirt.

Waiting for him to turn around so that she could change in the car, a frown appeared on her forehead.

"Advice? What advice?" she said twirling her finger for him to turn his back.

Standing guard, Anson tried to get a little mileage out of his studies. Rocking back and forth on his toes, he dug his hands into his pockets and simply said, "I looked under Apparel, as you suggested and it did say, in Deuteronomy 22:5, "women shall not wear that which pertained unto a man." Sounds like a dress is in order to me, right?" he laughed.

"Ugh. You knew and didn't tell me? We're supposed to be working together!" she pouted.

"I had my suspicions, Andie, but I needed more evidence to prove my theory. By the way, Triple combination means, the Bible, the Book of Mormon and the Doctrine and Covenants," he boasted.

"I knew that," she lied.

"Sure you did. You lie!" he teased.

"Men!" exasperatedly, she tilted her head and thought that she just couldn't admit that she was thankful that he was so diligent in his studies.

Now it was the moment of truth. How long could they pull off this charade? How long would it take until someone found them out? Only time would tell....

5 Moment of Truth

Andie and Anson entered the crowded Chapel and took their seats. Both raised in Christian homes, they could not help but compare this church with that which they had been raised.

"Pssst. Where are the statues? Why aren't there statues of Mary and Saint Peter and Jesus on a Cross?" Andie asked.

"From what I've been able to gather, they wish to think only of Jesus; concentrate the center of their lives on His existence. They believe that He will come again. It is not that they don't think that Mary was important or that Peter wasn't a great guy, it's just that those statues would detract from the real leader of the church, Jesus Christ. Did you even crack that book?" he asked nonchalantly.

"Okay, smarty. Why don't I see a big cross up there with Jesus hanging on it?" she asked quite sure that she had gotten his goat.

"Well, nice that you are so reverent about it," he whispered a sarcastic dig. "If we really loved Jesus the way we thought we were raised to, would you rather think about Him pessimistically up there, suffering on the cross? Or would you rather see Him in your mind's eye, raising the dead, performing miracles, being with children, and baptizing people? Get it? Positive, whilst knowing that He is here right now for you." He continued whispering, "They really believe that He is coming again. I think that is kind of neat, don't you?" he smiled as he listened to the speaker.

Andie looked straight ahead and then slowly turned towards Anson. Looking up at his smile, her stomach turned sour.

"Anson, you're not going soft on this are you? Did you forget that this is just an act? We're doing a job, that's all. Where did you *learn* all of this stuff, anyway? she whispered in a hushed demanding tone.

"Do you remember my talking about Bruiser? Look, see that big guy over there? That's him. When we were at Top Gun, he had already gone on his mission and he was still pretty hyped about the whole thing. He used to fill my ears with Mormon this and Mormon that, but I never really l listened. As I was reading on the plane, some of the things he had said started to fall into place, that's all. I'm just getting into my new job, Andie".

An older woman, trying in vain to hear the speaker, turned to see what the young couple were talking about in such hushed tones. She touched her hearing aid and smiled sweetly. What she was saying was, "please be respectful and listen," but her heart spoke the words even more gently.

As the Wellingss got ready to leave church, they were greeted by several young couples. It was overwhelming at best. All were wanting to know what each did for a living. When did they get married? How did they meet? Did they plan to have children soon? It was Andie's quick thinking that got them out of the jam.

"You know, we're still not settled yet in our little place, as a matter of fact, I really need to stock all my cupboards, but if you will all come over a week from next Friday at 7:00, we'll have a little open house and answer all your questions. By then, I'm sure we'll have the house in order. Is that alright with ya'll?" she flashed them a winning grin that they would not deny.

On the way out, Bruiser's wife Annette, stopped Andie. You know, two weeks is a long time to go without any new friends around. Wednesday, we're going down to the Bishop's Storehouse to fill some food orders. If you would like to come, we'd love the company!" she was so effervescently charming.

"You know, when we arrived, naturally the cupboards were absolutely bare. We've been eating out almost every meal. My list is so long that, I'm afraid the food would fill up your car!" she laughed.

"No food? But surely you mean.... oh! You ARE very funny! I can tell we are going to be great friends. For a minute there, I thought YOU needed the food for the underprivileged members, then when I remembered the amazing neighborhood you live in...Oh Andie, you are a kidder, just like me! My, it's going to be good to get a little fun back into this stuffy old ward," she continued laughing.

Andie hadn't realized right away that she had erred, but soon was laughing right along with Annette. *No problem, I've got this. I am going to get the hang of this Religion and*

53

its unusual jargon if it is the last thing I do on this planet.
That's the handbook I really needed to receive from the
Director, she thought, *Mormon Jargon!*

As they got home, they fell completely exhausted onto
the living room couches. They had been there almost four
hours and the time spent had been extremely intense. It
was so hard to keep up the façade of being a real Mormon!

They were mentally wiped out. Suddenly Anson got a
burst of energy from out of the blue. He jumped up and
started looking through closets. Andie followed him
curiously throughout the entire house as he would paw
through the items in the closets, close the door and proceed
to another. He kept mumbling the words, "They've got to
be here. They've got to be here somewhere!"

Finally, he looked where he should have looked first.
"Ah ha! I knew they wouldn't let me down! I knew Jack
wouldn't forget! Oh they're beautiful. I'm going to go try
these babies out. I'll see you later tonight," he said dragging
the prized item from the closet and practically ripping off
his suit as he ran up to his room.

"Anson, these are golf clubs!" she was aghast.

"Yeah, so what?" he stopped dead in his tracks.

"This is Sunday. You just can't go out and play golf on
Sunday. You are supposed to be observing the Sabbath.
You know, reading the scriptures, visiting the sick and doing
family things, remember? They talked about it in Sunday
School. It's right there in the Ten Commandments. Keep

the Sabbath Day Holy." It was clear she was confused, but her demeanor demanded an answer.

"Ah, Andie," he started, "I tried really hard. I was good and went to Church. I've been reading non-stop since we got the assignment. Now you've got to give me a little break, okay?" he pleaded.

"Anson, it's not for me to decide. I didn't give you the assignment, the Director did. He might as well be God. We have to do what he says. Remember?" She used her best imitation of the Director, "Read it, learn it, know it, live it! Sound familiar? True Mormons don't play golf or shop or do any work on Sunday," she was certain in her words. She could see now the defiant little boy in his demeanor.

Now, it wasn't that they had not been taught the Ten Commandments as children. That was evident by their knowledge of their existence. Now, the application of those Commandment to their lives would be more than mere words in the Bible.

"Are you sure? I mean, this could really cramp my style," he whined as he sat on the stairs.

"I tell you what," she started to climb the stairs. "I learned to play as a youngster. Why don't we set up a time with the Starter for next Saturday and I'll give you a run for your money?" she smiled as she patted him on the back.

"Really? You play golf AND shoot guns? You're some gal, Andie Wellings. I'm sorry. It was rather childish of me. It's just that there's so much pressure right now, and that's how I relieve it, by swinging at that darn little white ball!" he shook his head and covered his eyes.

Annie was just a step below him. She looked up at him with her big brown eyes and smiled, saying nothing but her eyes understanding all. Uncovering his eyes, he looked down and beamed.

"I guess we are really in this together, aren't we? Okay, we're supposed to be a family. What do families like us do all day Sunday after church?" he asked inquisitively.

"Well, it isn't like we can call someone up and ask them, can we?" Andie laughed. "You know we've studied probably more than most of the Church members do all month. Why don't we go for a walk and enjoy our community? Maybe we'll be able to meet some "neighbors" and do a little "missionary" work," she smiled slyly.

As they left the house, Anson took Andie's hand in his. She stopped for a brief moment and looked up into is eyes. With his free hand, he pushed back his blonde hair that had casually fallen forward, then gazed into her eyes and said coolly, "Remember, we have to act like we like each other in public."

Andie's heart throbbed so loudly for an instant that she was sure that he heard it. *No,* she thought, *the Director had said "more". I wonder if I will know when it isn't an act anymore?*

6 Neighbors

As the two strolled through the neighborhood, they decided to get their stories straight. It had been embarrassing at church when they could not answer the same questions exactly the same way.

"Let's see. I went to MIT for 18 months then went on a two-year mission to France. When I returned, I finished up at MIT and graduated when I was 25. You and I met...," he paused.

"We met at a Fraternity dance. I was an English Major at a local college. I have always had a secret desire to become a writer of children's novels," she stated.

"You have? Is that true or is that the story?" he wondered.

"Yes, other than defending my country from criminals, it's my very next dream," she said thoughtfully.

"Okay, we'd better get back to the story," he laughed. When I saw you at the dance, was it love at first sight?" he quizzed coyly.

"No, at first you hated me because I could dance better than you could," she smirked.

"Okay. I hear the subtle undertones in there. You are not going to let me forget about teasing you at the Academy, are you?" he asked.

"Not for a while. Forgiveness might be the call sign with real Mormons, but I'm still holding a few reservations," at least she was honest.

"Uh huh. If I have to "read it, know it, learn it and live it," so do you. I don't expect you to forgive me right away. I do expect you to hear where I was coming from. I just don't get it. Why law enforcement? You're good. I'll grant you that. No, you're fantastic, and intelligent. You have it all, Andie. Surely there was someone in your life?" Anson asked.

"I seem to intimidate every guy I meet. They don't see me as an equal, they see me as a road block. Something to knock down so they can climb over and get on with their lives," her voice started to shake.

"Hey I know sorry isn't good enough. I wasn't trying to pry. I just don't see why a woman would want to throw her life away chasing bad guys when she could have the world on a silver platter. You could, you know. You have to many talents, you could do anything with your life...," he began but she cut him off.

"But that is just it. I want to use my intelligence, my looks and my physical attributes to help protect the people of my Country. Why can't I find a guy who wants me for who I am?" she asked as they rounded the cul-de-sac on the other side of the street.

"Andie, I am afraid that there are just too many guys who don't want to lay awake at night wondering if some terrorist has his wife at knifepoint," he said, turning to her and lifting her chin. "I think I am one of them," he gently kissed her.

"Well," spoke the voice from the neighbor's garden, "you must be the two newlyweds who moved in across the street. At least you ACT like newlyweds!" he laughed.

Anson and Andie gasped in surprise and giggled quietly in their embarrassment as their audience rose from his flowers and took off his gardening gloves to shake their hands. *How much had he heard?*

"I'm John Smithe. You've chosen a really nice neighborhood. We have block parties during the summer up in the cul-d-sac. Everyone is pretty tight. If you ever need anything right away, we all run to each other's rescue. Enough about me. How long have you two lovebirds been married?" he asked.

The two answered at once and then stumbled over each other's words in the confusion.

"Seven...," said Anson.

"...teen," said Andie.

"we...," said Anson.

"Months!" Andie blurted. "Oh you know how it is, Mr. Smithe. First, we were counting the hours, then days and weeks. We just can't believe we're into months now," Andie smoothed over the rumples.

"Andie, has it really been almost a year and a half? I can't believe how fast time flies," Anson put his arm around her waist.

"My husband is incurable romantic, Mr. Smithe. He wants babies right now and I want to be a famous writer first. I just can't seem to persuade him differently," she said flashing him a smile.

"Well, there's a lot to be said for that Mrs.....?" he began.

"Wellings. Just call me Andie. This is Anson."

"Well Andie, we only have one but she brings a lot of joy into our lives. They are so inquisitive. I hope our little Faith doesn't intrude too much on your privacy. She is a very precocious and curious child and loves to talk," he laughed.

"Not at all. I'm home during the days, I'd probably enjoy the company once in a while. Does your wife work?" Andie's timing was perfect.

"No. She stays at home. She hasn't been well of late. She plays a little tennis and golf at the club and works on charity events. Where will you be working Anson?" he changed the subject.

"I've taken a position at Northrup. It's really a transfer. I was with the Louisiana Division," he smiled.

"Really! You're the one, huh?" he sized him up putting his finger on his chin. "Somehow, I pictured you to be older," he nodded.

"Pardon me?" Anson couldn't believe his ears. Had his cover been blown already?

"Yep. They said they were bringing a specialist in from Louisiana, but somehow that brings to mind grey hair and a cane!" he sighed. "Makes me feel a little old. You can't be more than 35," he surmised.

"You're only off by one year. I spent six years in the Navy after I received my Masters. Been a loyal employee for almost 5 years working in R and D. That's Research and Development. They seem to think I know how to help them with a project or two. Wait, YOU work there too?" he concluded easily.

"Yeah. I've moved up quite a bit in eight years, now I basically head up Contracts and Negotiations. Get to work with the main people. It's pretty exciting. It's one thing to make the part, but to see it be put into action and directly affect peoples' lives is quite another," he said.

I'll bet. I'm ready to find out how you do it too, Anson nodded smiling.

"I haven't seen the main operation. Do you think I could follow you in to work tomorrow?" Anson baited.

"Better yet, why don't we ride together. That is, if we have the same shift. I work from 7:30 to 4:30. I requested those hours so that I could be home in the afternoon with Faith," he added.

"I honestly don't know what my hours are going to be yet," Anson lied. "Didn't you mention that your wife is home during the day?"

"My wife is not always in the best of health and we don't like to let Faith go unsupervised. I help out whenever I can and I have a woman who comes in and helps out with the homework," he said.

"I'm sorry. I guess I have a mixed picture in my mind. I could have sworn that you said she played tennis and golf. Sounded pretty healthy to me," Anson peered into John's eyes.

"It's one of those things that comes and goes. Listen, tomorrow you follow me. They'll tell you what schedule you'll be on. We'll play it by ear, okay?" he asked.

"Sure I'll be out here at what, 7:00?" he didn't know exactly how far they would have to travel.

"Sounds good. Until then. Mrs. Wellings, nice to make your acquaintance," he charmed.

"Andie. Just call me Andie. I'm still not used to Mrs. Wellings. It sounds like I'm Anson's Mother," she laughed.

After parting, Anson did not take his arm off of her waist. They took the long way around the cul-d-sac instead of merely crossing the street. Andie was secretly glad, it felt good to be in Anson's arms, under his protection. Even though she could protect herself, there was a sense of satisfaction that everything was perfect, or was it still an act?

"Seems like an awfully nice guy. I feel funny almost busting someone that nice, with a family," she added.

"It's a shame about white collar crime. Most executives that get caught with their fingers in the cookie jar are only trying to watch out for their families' best interest. Greed takes a hold of their better judgement and crime gets the upper hand in their list of priorities," he shook his head sadly.

"That's our job; ridding the world of crime and making it a fair place for everyone to live. It seems so idealistic. I wonder if we will ever get ahead of it all," she sighed.

"When we took the oath, they never said that all of the crooks we were going to catch would be filthy, slimy, unshaven animals with no respect for authority. There will be youth. There will be housewives and nice husbands who merely took the wrong path. All we can do is halt their activities and help them choose the right path later," he said.

"Yeah, and try not to get killed in the meantime. Did you mean what you said about not wanting your wife on the other end of a knife or gun?" she asked.

"That's a stupid question for someone as smart as you, Andie," he smiled as he rumpled her short brown hair.

They walked up to their doorstep and he opened the door for her.

"Such a gentleman. I guess I didn't phrase it right. This whole thing is getting me quite confused, Anson. It's difficult for me to sort out my feelings for you as a friend and a co-worker," she added.

"An   d...that's all? I must admit. I'm starting to have marbles swimming around in my head too. I feel this need to concentrate on our job, on getting the man who is betraying our Country. Then, I look at you doing something around the house and it feels so comfortable here. It feels right.," he closed the door and kissed her.

"I feel dizzy, she said fanning her face.

"I didn't know I had that effect on women," he smiled.

"You know; you don't have to...you know ...the door's closed. I   mean, we're not in public now. You don't have to act like you like me now, if you don't want to," she stammered.

"That's just it, tousle head," he rumpled her hair again and stroked her neck then pulled her to him. "I do like you. I like you a lot," and kissed her forehead.

"You do?" she whimpered then pulled herself together. "Well, Mr. Wellings, you'd better pull yourself together and get on with getting this guy, then we can explore future options, okay?" she teased, holding onto his tie and leading him up to his room.

"Okay, but listen. I would never do anything against your will. Believe me, I of all people know your capabilities. I would feel more comfortable if you kept your door locked at night," he smiled lazily.

"The way you kiss, you'd better keep your door locked," she raised her eyebrows and closed the door.

Anson waltzed dreamily to his room and closed the door quietly. He felt silly with confusion. Suddenly, as if snapped from a trance, his logical mind started rapid firing questions.

What's wrong with me? What are my directives? Where are my priorities? I've got to get a grip on myself. My whole future is at stake with this job.

Sure, it was easy to make these decisions. The doors were locked.

7 The Executive

The next morning, Anson arose promptly at five and put on his jogging clothes. This was a habit he had gotten into while at the Academy. He didn't like it, but it was good for him. As he left his room, he was surprised to see Andie doing the same.

"Hey, this is great! I didn't know you were still into jogging?" he smiled.

"I'm not. It's a necessary evil. I run. There's a big difference. It's easier on the heart and you get in shape faster. You should try that. That is," she smiled, "if you can keep up with me," she laughed as she raced down the stairs.

"But, I thought that a nice slow 5-mile jog would really start me off right, he stammered clambering down the stairs after her.

"Basically, I start off with some warm up exercises like this," she demonstrated a few. "You DO warm ups, don't you? You could really pull a hamstring if you don't, you know?" she became more serious.

"Yes. Of course," he halfheartedly did some warm ups just to please her. "Okay! There's no way that I can run full tilt for five miles! Okay? So there. You've got me," he confessed.

"Anson, I don't go full speed for five miles. I run a quarter, then walk a quarter. Then I run a half and walk a half. Then I build to 3/4, walking and running. Finally, I taper off all the way back down to a quarter to cool down. Come on. I'll go easy on you," she opened the door.

"Listen, about last night," he started.

"I know. Anson we're not falling in love with each other, are we? I mean, it would ruin a perfectly good friendship and partnership, I think. It must be just the situation we're in. It's easy to fall in love with a situation," she insisted.

"Yes. That's it. You must admit, it's pretty romantic. A new house, a   beautiful wife, a perfect job, two beautiful cars, gorgeous furniture," he sighed. "It's all going to vanish when it's over, isn't it?" he asked sadly.

"Yep. Do you really think that I'm beautiful?" she curiously tilted her head.

"I'll race you to that tree," he quickly changed the subject.

When they returned, Anson took off his soiled clothes and placed them into the hamper in the bathroom. Then before entering the shower, he wrapped himself in a towel and meticulously laid out every item that he would be wearing to work. Surveying the situation like an engineer admires the bridge that he just built, Anson gave himself a nod of approval and bounded off to the shower.

Andie, was a different breed of cat. She dropped her dirty sweats somewhat near the piles of things she had worn the other night. She had always been like that. Even as a child, her idea of cleaning her room was to shove everything under the bed. She could only take it for so long then would get frustrated and clean it up perfectly.

Pulling open a drawer, she peered inside. Everything that she deemed "relaxing clothes" were unfolded and shoved in as quickly as possible. She grabbed that which she needed for the day and bounced off to her own shower.

Bess Castle was waiting for them in the kitchen. She looked at the two as they entered the Dutch door to the kitchen simultaneously. Her, in a pair of bike shorts and a T-shirt and he, dressed quite handsomely in his navy pinstripe suit.

"My, Mr. Wellings, you do cut a dashing figure in that suit," she admired.

"Yes, you do look pretty nice, except....," Andie hesitated.

"Except what?" he demanded to know.

"Oh, nothing," she looked down at the oatmeal and plate of cut fruit placed before her.

"You were going to say that something wasn't right. By George, tell me! Don't let me go off to work with my confidence hanging on an "Oh, nothing...." "Now, what?" he needed to know.

"Well, it's that tie," she started

"What's wrong with my tie? This is a perfectly good tie. My Mother helped me pick it out," he spoke curtly.

"Does your mother always help you pick out mismatched ties?" she wondered.

"No, I do that all by myself. I mean, usually. I mean, it was just that once and I couldn't hurt her feelings," he stated.

"Do you have to wear it when she's not around or just when she comes to visit?" Andie asked waving a forkful of melon.

"No, you're trying to be cute. Alright. I'll change the tie. To what? What should I change it to?" he asked.

"Something solid and something not too bold. Burgundy or Grey, even gold, but not those ridiculous green and black polka dots. It makes me want to lose my breakfast," she laughed.

"Great. Anything else? You seem to be the fashion coordinator around here," he humored her.

"Stand up. Turn around. Uh, huh. The shoes have got to go. You can't wear brown wingtips with a navy suit. Do you have black...anything?" she asked seriously.

"Yes. Black wingtips. I'll be right back," he smiled.

When he returned, he presented himself with a much more professional look. He was genuinely pleased with himself for the new knowledge he had attained.

"Well, what do you think?" he asked.

"Oh my!" said Mrs. Castle, shaking her hand in the air.

"Much better," Andie nodded her vote of approval.

"Thank you. My roommates used to just laugh at what I put on. They never offered any constructive criticism," he smiled as he finished his last bite of breakfast.
"That's okay. You've got a pretty okay looking body in that suit. Why ruin it with the wrong accessories?" she spoke truthfully as she walked him to the door and opened it for him.

"Really, you think I've got a good body?" he asked standing on the porch.

"Go to work," she closed the door right in his face as she shook her head and smiled.

Anson knocked on the door.

Andie opened the door and peered into a very confused face. "What is it?" she wanted to know.

"Well, Mr. Smithe is standing over there on the walk way, and I was wondering if you could just kiss me good-bye, you know, for appearance sake," he was wringing his hands.

Andie took a step out onto the porch and wrapped her arms around his neck.

"You mean; you want me to act like a "beautiful" wife?" she teased.

"Yeah, I guess so," he smiled sheepishly.

"Anything for the FBI, Anson," she smiled and planted a very wet kiss on his lips. "There, that ought to do it," she stepped back and started to close the door. "Bye, darling. Have a nice day!" she called just loud enough for any passer-by to hear.

Anson tried to remain calm as he walked to the car, but his heart was clearly racing. *Keep your mind on the job, Wellings! Remember the directive.* He bit his lip to encourage sane thoughts to keep from flying around in his head and settle down. It worked, for now.

8 Clocking in

"Good morning! Better enjoy that while it lasts," John smiled, shaking Anson's hand before unlocking the car door for him.

"While it lasts?" asked Anson.

"After about 10 years, you'll have to lay out your own clothes, get your own breakfast and blow her a kiss while she sleeps in," he laughed.

"Oh, this could mean trouble. I already lay out my own clothes!" Anson teased back.

"It only takes about seven minutes to get to the office from here. Nervous?" John asked.

"A little. New surroundings, new expectations. I just hope I am able to live up to what they expect. I've got to do that in a job. I can't be happy being a robot; have to feel like I am contributing," Anson sighed a believable sigh.

"I know what you mean. You'll like O'Rourke. He's a real team player. That's probably who you'll be seeing first. He'll get you started and tell you who you will be working with. It's the next exit," John flashed his turning signal as he exited the freeway.

"Is there anyone I have to look out for? There's always some cutthroat who is vying for the top dog position," he wondered.

"That would be Miss Van Briggle, "O'Rourke's bull dog secretary. She's very protective of him and extremely snoopy. I can't make a move around that place without her looking over my shoulder. Just do your job and don't gossip with anyone or she'll find out and use it against you," he warned.

Pulling up at the gate, the Security Guard could see that Anson was not wearing a Security Badge. He asked him to get out of the car and come over to the gate.

"I'm Anson Wellings. I believe Mr. O'Rourke is expecting me," Anson explained.

"Mr. Wellings, I'm Joe Daniels. I've been briefed on your operation here. It really ticks me off that something got leaked. It better not have been through my gate, or I'll have the guy's head. If you feel you need to carry, you just make sure you always enter and leave through my gate and not the others. You have top Security clearance here, sir," he explained quietly.

"Thank you Joe," said Anson, knowing that "carry" meant he was given carte blanche permission to defend himself with his weapon if necessary. "The less people knowing the reason for my visit, the better," he said as he received his new badge. As they walked back to the car, Joe asked John to walk Anson to Mr. O'Rourke's office personally.

"He likes you well enough," John spoke freely. "He really takes his job seriously sometimes," he continued.

"Good. We need more men like him. There's a lot of secrets lurking within these walls. I'd hate to see if any leak out," Anson spoke cautiously.

"Yeah, that's right," John shot a glance at Anson for a split second.

Mike O'Rourke was a tall man with a tinge of grey at the temples.

The very thought of espionage is going on right under my nose is more than I can handle. He got up and eagerly greeted Anson as he entered his office.

"Glad to meet you, Mr. Wellings. You come very highly recommended. I can't tell you how this thing has me shook up. When the Director of the FBI called me and told me what their intelligence had discovered, I felt so guilty that I hadn't done more Security wise. You know, I just couldn't believe it, what with the spirit of Glasnost and whatnot. I thought when the wall came down, we didn't have to worry about spies anymore," he apologized.

"Now that the walls are beginning to crumble, we must be on our guard more than ever, Mr. O'Rourke. Espionage has been around since the beginning of time, and we hardly think that it will stop because of some Goodwill gestures. Of course, it's wonderful to see Democracy blossoming all around the world, but where would we be if we took a non-aggressive posture and took all of our people out of Russia, or China or wherever Communism exists? We need to know as many secrets as they have and they will always try to find out ours. That's our game. You shouldn't feel guilty. I've been told that your Security is top notch. It's just that they can be very crafty. It's their business to do so. It's my business to stop them," Anson spoke articulately.

"Well, we want to catch them in the act, but we don't want a diplomatic scandal. We'll never be trusted again with another Government Contract. It's imperative that they don't get the cloaking device. DC is giving us a chance to clean our own house. Somehow, we've got to let them think that they received it, catch them passing it off and then arrest the proper parties. For Perestroika's sake, the government wants to slap as few hands as possible. They just want to deport anyone involved and prosecute any American citizens. Do you think that you can pull this off?" Mike asked.

"It's what I've been trained to do, sir," Anson said confidently. "Where would you like me to begin?" he inquired.

"I'm putting you in Research, but not as Head. You'll work as Assistant to Dr. Joan Brennery. She's tops in her field. She knows all about you. As a matter of fact, she is the one who designed it," he concluded as there was a knock on the door.

Before he opened the locked passageway, he said, "Anson, I will expect you to keep me fully posted. I want to know how this could happen under my nose."

The door opened and in walked Joan Brennery, Ph.D. Her light brown hair was tied neatly back in a ponytail. Her ivory face was framed by tortoise shell glasses.

"I take it, you're Wellings. I worked too hard on this project to let it go down the drain. I want you to find the traitor who is selling us out," she demanded, clutching her clipboard. "It's got to be Smithe. He's the one who has had the most access. It's just logic that the blame should fall on him," she announced.

Suppose he is being framed? Is it possible that he is just the fall guy and there are others involved?" Anson asked That's why you're here. We've done briefcase checks for the past two weeks and have found virtually nothing of significant importance. We even have the people pass through a metal detector to see if computer chips are being transferred covertly or on their bodies. You figure it out. It's out of my league. If he is being blackmailed, that is one thing, if he is being tortured or something is happening with his family, that's one thing, but to just flagrantly hand over our Top Secret Innovations...well...I want to see him fry for that!" Joan demanded.

"I can understand why you are upset. When you go to all that work and research, it's nice to be able to take credit for something as brilliant as this," Anson charmed.

That drew a smile from Joan. "You recognize this as brilliant, hmmm? Maybe you're not just Deputy Dawg after all," she laughed. "Come on. I'll show you the lab. You've certainly got the clearance for it. Now let's see if you have the aptitude to grasp the concepts. The place is just bug proof. We can talk more there," she flashed him a grin.

"Anson, good luck," Mike shook his hand. "We're counting on you."

"Thank you, sir. I'll keep you posted," Anson promised.

9 Dream Lab

The lab was a giant room, the size of a small airplane hangar. It was filled with prototypes and miniatures of different aeronautical projects. The lab was sparsely dotted with white coated figures, all wearing the coveted purple Top Secret Clearance badges.

Once safely inside the airlock, Joan spoke frankly. "I thought you'd never get here. This has been quite fraying to my nerves. I apologize for jumping on your case back there," she said holding her hand outstretched.

Anson clasped it. *Another female to work with. What lesson is God trying to teach me?*

"Apology accepted, Doctor Joan," he smiled.

"Now would you like a tour?" she asked.

"Of course! What is the procedure when something needs to be accomplished?" he wondered.

"You mean when we get a Government Contract? First, we collect the necessary specifications that are required to bid on the project. Several other companies receive the same specs, which is when things usually get leaked to the press. They find out that the Government is trying to find someone to build something for them. Then, we design whatever it is based on what their needs are and submit it in a contract form with blueprints. Once negotiations are completed, contracts are signed, the building and testing is begun. The adversaries have been getting an idea of what we are going to do before we ever get to build it," she said.

"That's what you meant about Smithe. He's letting them have copies of the contracts. What about copies of the blueprints?" he asked.

"We don't know that for a fact that this is what he is doing. We only suspect. It is against company policy to let blue prints leave the building. If we did that, anyone could grab the bid. But, they somehow have gathered intelligence to suggest that the Russians actually have copies of several major project blue prints. That's how we know it's an inside job. We've been feeding the C and N division phony projects for the past two weeks, but we can't operate on a positive cash flow for very long this way," she concluded.

"How does it work? The cloaking device, I mean. How are you able to make a bomber or any plane disappear for that matter," he asked?

"Let me show you. Radar is nothing more that sound waves bouncing off the ground, up to a target, and back down to the ground. Advanced tracking devices also detect heat from the vapor trails. My technique allows for the radar beam pass right through the ship, virtually undetected. The object is still visible to the eye, but undetectable by radar," she was clearly excited about the system.

"Can you show me how?" he asked.

"Sure. First, we reconstructed the hull of the ship. We filled it with a layer of wires that transmit a steady flow of negative ions throughout the vessel. Spraying from the nose of the craft, on the outside, is a mixture of liquid nitrogen, silver nitrate and a mixture of coolants that form a cloud of fog around the ship. Near the exhaust system, the majority of the cloud is emitted forcing the vapor trail to cool instantly," she said.

"Ingenious. How many years have you been working on this?" he wanted to know.

"About six. It's always been a dream of mine, before they even requested such a device. So you see, with six years of my life invested in this one project alone, I'm sure you can identify with my frustration," she concluded.

"Well, it gives me something to think about. What do I do first?" he asked.

"For the first week or so, why don't you just carry around this clipboard and see if you can jot down any firm information that seems suspicious to you," she said.

"Thanks. Here's your special badge. You'll need that in addition to the one you've already got to get you in here. "Don't let it out of your sight," she added.

"Okay. I'll try to stay out of your way as much as possible," he said.

"Anytime you have something to report, just ask me if I'm going to take a coffee break soon. I never take breaks, even though I should. They say that it increases productivity and all...anyway, just ask me and I'll know." With that, she had formulated their secret code.

The ride home seemed to take longer than seven minutes. Anson was tired from so much input in one day. John wanted to know how his day had been and if he liked it.

"I liked it well enough. The things that this lab is working on is phenomenal. I'm sorry, I can't discuss it with anyone, but I sure wish we had had Dr. Brennery at the other facility. I'd like to kick myself for wasting all those years under yo-yos that call themselves Ph.Ds. They just thought they were creating things. Joan is discovering true scientific breakthrough," Anson was excited.

"Oh yeah? Like what, in particularly?" John primed the pump.

"Well, I don't think I am allowed to talk to you about it. I'm sorry. I am only cleared to discuss those things within the lab itself," he said apologetically.

"Sure, I understand," he said. "I have limited clearance. The hard part is not talking to the wife about things that you see that are of great importance, huh?" he wanted to know just how far Anson's loyalties went.

"That's for sure. Especially when you are involved with things which are of a sensitive nature, purely Top Secret. She always drills me. You'd think she worked for the Russians," he laughed easily.

"Don't they all?" John laughed too as they entered the driveway of his house. "See you tomorrow. Are we on the same schedule?" John asked.

"Yep. We sure are. Thanks. I'll alternate with you next week on the driving, okay?" Anson asked.
"The company will be good," John said.

10 Curious little girl

Andie sat in the surveillance room, waiting for more activity. She was bored. The camera had buzzed on a few times. Once for the mailman. Once for a television repair truck and sporadically flashed on and off during the hours that the little girl was home from school.

Andie looked beyond the sheer curtains to see the child sitting on the curb staring at the Wellings home. She looked so intently at Andie's window. She didn't break her stare, yet she looked lonely. It touched Andie's heart that when all was said and done, the child's father would be taken from her and tried as a traitor. Hopefully, the mother would be able to get straightened out and give her child a good life; one that she deserved.

Glancing back at the computer screen, Andie played with the keys in anticipation of beginning her first novel. She needed a character. Thoughts were flying like spray paint in her brain.

A woman. That's it. A young, independent woman who...needs a man. No, a young, independent, beautiful woman, who needs a job. No, a young, independent beautiful woman, who is bored out of her mind and would rather be out chasing crooks than sitting at the dumb computer writing novels that no one will ever read. That's it. That's my character!

She peered past the edge of the monitor, only to see the little girl, still there, with her chin on her hands staring back at her. Andi could see out through the darkened glass, but it was unquestionably impossible to see in. Suddenly she could stand it no more.

Andie slapped her hands upon the desk in finality of Chapter One and arose majestically. She marched downstairs and opened the front door.

"Little girl! Yes. You! Can you come here?" she asked. The child raced with glee to meet Andie. Her face literally beamed with excitement.

"I was praying that you would come out, and you DID!" she squealed with delight.

"I saw you and I wanted...," before Andie could finish, this child with a voice quicker than lightening spoke.

"My name is Faith. I'm 8, no, I'm 8 and ten twelfths to be exact. I live right over there in that house. I wasn't supposed to come over and hug you unless you invited me. You DID and so here I am! Can I come in? Do you want to play jump rope with me? I am really good at jump rope. Do you want to play?" she beamed.

"Faith. What a glorious name. Just one thing, okay? Slow, down. You are taking my breath away." Andie laughed.

"Oh. I'm sorry. I do that. I don't mean to. I just get excited. Do you want me to leave? Of course you do. Okay," she moped dejectedly towards the door. "Please don't tell my father that I bothered you," she turned and started to go home.

"Wait! There you go again. You just move a little quicker than I am used to. Come in please. I've met your Dad. He's a wonderful guy. He thought you might like to keep me company sometimes," she smiled.

"Really? Like right now? I'd love to. What do you want me to do? I'll do anything. I can clean, vacuum mend clothes, you just name it," she chimed.

"Hold on. I can't play every day, but I'm stuck for some ideas for my book. I thought I'd make Anson some peanut butter cookies. Do you want to help me?" Andie asked.

"Would I? Of course! Anything beats sitting over at my house. We have a really grouchy maid, named Eve. She wears a fake blonde wig and she's a lousy housekeeper and can't cook. She doesn't like me. I don't think she likes any children for that matter. She's mean to my mom too.," she shook her head.

Andie was being a good listener. She wondered what else might slip out if she played her cards right. She flipped on her remote computer monitor in the kitchen. On the screen flashed her outline format for different characters. She glanced at it as she went to the cupboard. Opening the pantry, Faith peered into it in a nosy little way.
    "My goodness. I've never seen so much good in all my life. Are you sure that there are only two of you here?

There's enough food for all the starving children in Africa!" Faith exclaimed.

"I guess I went a little crazy at the store, huh? I hope we're not on any sort of food budget," she wondered out loud.

"You mean you don't <u>know</u>? You really haven't been married very long. At our house, it's budget this and budget that. Turn off the lights, don't let the water drip, don't use the air conditioner unless you are absolutely "dying." That's what I hear all the time," she said.

"Really? I thought your parents were doing pretty well. This is a nice neighborhood and all...," she asked wondering what other secrets Faith held dear.

"No. Don't worry, you'll learn to say all of that too. I think it comes with being a mom. All my friends hear that too. It just comes with the territory," she answered.

"Oh, I see. You're right. I've just got to get in there and learn the ropes. I supposed you'll be glad to help me, hmm?" she smiled as she got out the mixing bowl.

"Here, crack these two eggs. I have to get the phone," she said, changing the subject.

It was the Bishop. He needed to meet with Anson and Andie at the building. Ordinarily, the secretary set up the appointment, but this was special, he said.

"Okay. Tomorrow night at 7:30? We'll be there," she smiled as she replaced the phone on the hook.

"We were talking about babies," Faith reminded her.

"No. We were not. Not for a while, at least!" Andie tossed the egg shells into the sink.

"Don't you like kids?" Faith frowned.

"No, it's not that. We just got married. We've got to get to know each other a little bit before we start to know another little being, don't you think?" she smiled.

"But you are Mormons. I know you're Mormons because Sandy Elliott, who is in my class, goes to your church. You Mormons, like to have lots of babies around. Sandy said, they are like gifts from God and you are the caretakers of their spirits while they are on Earth. I think that is nice and I think that you should have twins right away," she insisted.

"Well, you'll have to talk to Anson about that. I'm sure he'll get a real charge out of it. But, we've really not been married long enough, dear," Andie popped the tray into the waiting oven.

"Ok. How long have you been married?" she persisted.

Only about five days, Andie mused in her mind.

"Well, I guess it's almost 18 months now," Andie smiled at her perseverance.

"I can add. It only takes 9 months to have a baby. You could have had two children by now. 9 times 2 is 18. Simple really. You should have taken that first nine months to get to know him while you were waiting for the baby while you were waiting for a second baby." She sounded amazed that a College graduate like Andie didn't know better.

"I can't believe I didn't think about that!" Andie gave up trying to reason.

The front door opened and closed as Anson quickly approached the swinging doors to the entrance of the kitchen.

"Andie?" he called to her.

"Here in the kitchen. We have a guest," she warned.

"Guest? Well, who are you, little lass?" he bellowed.

"This is Faith, dear. You know, the neighbor's girl? I believe their last name is Smithe, remember?" she smiled.

"Faith. Such a pretty name. What are you two girls up to? Where's my dinner?" he smiled.

"Well, we made you some cookies instead. Aren't you going to kiss her?" Faith asked.

"Pardon me?" Anson was taken aback. Andie burst into giggles.

"Yes, all husbands kiss their wives. You're not gay are you? Is that why you don't have any babies yet?" Faith continued.

"Excuse me. I'll do my duty, Miss Smithe," he saluted then took
Andie into his arms and gave her a little peck on the cheek.

"That wasn't a very good one. You'd better try again or she's going to divorce you," Faith persisted.

"I beg your pardon," he obeyed.

It was clear that he liked taking orders from the eight-year-old. The next kiss was entirely more passionate. Andie looked almost dizzy when he finished this one. Andie, however was getting a little tired of Faith's routine and was worried that soon the subject would change to that of baby...

"That was better. But you'll have to try harder. You need about 1,998 more for a girl baby. Only 998 more for a boy. I know these things." She was clearly an authority on the matter.

"Is that so?" Anson humored her as Andie covered her eyes with her hand as she sat down to the table.

"Tell me more, Faith. Just how long have you had this theory?" he chided, eating one of their cookies.

"Oh, forever. Well, you'd better get started. I've got to go home for dinner. Bye Andie," she said. Then pulling her close, she whispered, "I like him. He's cute," and ran out the door giggling.

"I like that girl. She's got enterprising ideas. Going to go far in the world, I'd say," he laughed.

"I don't think she stopped talking the whole time she was here. I may go mad before I'm through," she laughed.

"Listen. I've got to tell you. I got the royal treatment today and Dr. Joan is just fantastic. I'm really going to love working with her. She's bright, intelligent, innovating, beautiful," he beamed then looked down to see that she wasn't really listening, but paying attention to her computer monitor.

"Character one: Eve Lindell

Hair: Blonde

Eyes:

I don't know. I like the first name, but I'll have to think up a more dramatic last name. We have a meeting tomorrow night with the Bishop at 7:30. Did you say you are working with a beautiful woman?" she sounded blasé.

"Well, in a generic sort of way. Her scientific soul speaks to mine," he said, trying to make her jealous.

"That's nice. The two of you should be very happy together," she monotone as she stared at the computer, trying not to show any emotion. "But you might try to remember that you're a married man. A married Mormon man who sets a good example in the community, that's all."

"Of course. I knew that," he lied as he poured himself a bowl of cold cereal for dinner.

11 Bishop Knows...

The next day was already pretty routine for Anson. He took notes of different things around the building, but nothing was suspicious enough to warrant a special meeting with Dr. Brennery.

Andie got a little more work done on her book, then took her beeper out to the pool. She wanted to be ready to go up and check out any activity. The buzzer never rang as she did her laps. Only upon reentering the house did she get a phone call from little Faith.

"I know you are expecting me," her voice sounded strange, "but I'm sick and can't come out for a while."

"Oh Faith. I hope it's nothing serious. How is your mother? Is she able to help you?" Andie wanted to meet her soon.

"Yeah, as much as she can. She likes to be alone sometimes. She gets bruises. I'll be alright, really. I have to go, she's coming," she whimpered.

"Bruises? What do you mean? Call me if there is anything I can do, really," Andie insisted as she set the phone down.

The rest of the day, she spent wondering what to wear when she saw the Bishop and trying to decipher Faith's message. She needed more evidence that John was abusing his wife. Where else would she get bruises? Before long,

Anson arrived and they were ready to go to the Chapel to meet with him.

"Brother and Sister Wellings. How good of you to come," he smiled.

"We're glad to meet you, sir," they both smiled as they sat down.

"The purpose of this interview is just to meet with you and get acquainted and possibly to extend a calling," he said.

After they began with a word of prayer, which both Andie and Anson proudly folded their arms for, Anson was the first to speak.

"Did you say calling? What is that exactly?" he was puzzled.

"You know, a job in the church," the Bishop smiled.

"Oh, thank you. We're fine, really. I've got a really good job at Northrup and Andie works at home," he said proudly answering the first question with flying colors.

"Oh, I thought I saw you the other day. I work there too. I'm sure that you know that the jobs in the church aren't for money, but for blessings. Ah, but someone told me that you two really are quite the comedians. You really had me going there," the Bishop chuckled.

"Anson, I'd like you to be the Sunday School teacher for the 13 year olds," he smiled.

"Oh, thank you, really. I, uh, don't think so. I'm not sure that I know enough...I'm good.," Anson began but Andie cut him off as she stepped on his toe.

"What Anson means is that he is not sure that he could handle the 13 year olds. Sure he studies every day, but that's a pretty demanding group. Do you have any groups a little younger that he could choose from?" she asked.

"Well, Sister Wellings. I'm sure you well know that when we ask someone to take a calling, we've already prayed about it and pretty much received an answer from the Lord. However, if you would like me to go back and pray about it again...," he hesitated.

"Oh, no. I'm sorry. I didn't mean to interfere. I was only trying to help," she answered apologetically.

"Do I have to accept this.... uh...calling?" Anson paused.

"Of course not. I'd like you to go home and pray about it also. I had heard that you were on a Mission. France, was it? I'm sure you have many exciting stories to tell the kids. You're still a young man, you know. They really like young teachers. Perhaps it's because they can relate with them and try to emulate them. Please let me know," he added.

"Thank you," Anson breathed a sigh of relief and sat back.

"Now about Temple Recommends," he waited for their reply with eyebrows raised.

"Uh. I don't know, honey. What do you think? Do you know of any that you could recommend?" Anson was stuck. He was drowning and begging for a rope.

"Let's see," she chimed in, "there's the one in Oakland. I heard it has beautiful golden spires that light up at night on the hill. Breathtaking. I would certainly recommend that one. And then there's one in Salt Lake City, Utah. It's supposed to be pretty nice to visit," she smiled knowing she had aced that question.

"Uh...huh.... Is there anything you two would like to get off your chests? Anything at all? The Bishop's eyes seemed to look straight into their souls.

"Nope," said Anson as he twiddled his fingers in his lap.

"Uh...no...not that comes to mind," said Andie, gulping hard.

"I just want you to know that I'm here anytime you want to talk. Really. You can talk to me about anything and it won't leave this room. I'm here to help you," he said in a comforting manner. "Shall we have a word of prayer?" he asked.

"Do I have to give it?" Anson asked with fear frozen on his face.

"Of course not," the kindly Bishop, again smiled and offered a word of prayer.

In the prayer, he asked that whatever transgressions these two might have committed be forgiven so they could return to the Temple soon. He invited the Spirit of the Holy Ghost to give them the courage to talk about whatever it was that was bothering them. He asked Heavenly Father to guard them from harm and then the Bishop thanked Him for sending them to his ward.

When they left, Andie was in tears. Anson was moved. They shook hands and parted, promising to come back and talk at length someday soon.

In the parking lot, Andie stopped in her tracks. "How does he know? He looked right through us. I wanted to spill my guts."

"Me too. You know of course, that he knows everything. I really tried to answer those questions as well as I could but I could see it in his eyes, they were trick questions. He knows we are fakes. We've totally blown our cover," he said sadly.

"Yeah, I know. I felt it too. He's a very special guy, you know? I think he wanted to help us but wants it to be our decision," she added.

"The Bureau needs him in their interrogation room. He could suck more secret codes out of...," Anson began and was cut off by Andie.

"Anson, I feel so guilty. Everything that I learned about this Church is true. I know it. I want to go back and tell him everything. I'm sure that he will help us. Don't you think?" she asked honestly and openly.

"Andie," he put his arm around her shoulders. I'm feeling so confused. I really don't know what to do. Everything I've read in the Book of Mormon makes perfect sense. I know in my heart that it's the true Second Witness of Jesus Christ. I am sure now, that when Jesus was resurrected, for that time, before he ascended into Heaven, he really did have other flocks to visit. I think that is how he was able to beam himself over to South America and visit the Lamanites. How else would they have detailed information about a white man coming to visit them? They described him perfectly and the time frame coincides exactly," he explained.

"Beamed?" she laughed, "Like Star Trek "beamed?" "Yeah," he quipped, "maybe but what are you confused about? Do you want to be baptized?" she asked hoping his answer was the same as hers.

"Yes and no. Yes, I do, but not now. The timing is just so messed up. We've got to concentrate on what it is we're supposed to do. When I get up the courage, maybe I will tell the Bishop what's going on. After all, he did say that anything we said would be held in confidence," he sighed.

"The buzzer sounded in the First Counselor's office next door to the Bishop's. Bruiser touched the button in reply.

"Vaughn? Could you come in here a moment?" he asked

"Yes, Bishop? What can I do for you?"

"Just wondering if you've had a chance to meet the Wellingss. Have you noticed any out of the unusual?" He began gathering information on his own without letting on to his counselor what he had suspected all along.

12 Covert Activity

Two weeks had flown by and it was time to make good on a promise. This was the Friday night that they were to have a party. Andie was at home, making last minute consultations with the Cosmic Caterers whom she had hired through the Bureau. Everyone was coming, including the Smithes, Inez and Jack Gibbens had just been invited moments ago.

Anson had just called Andie and nervously said, "Honey, don't forget to invite Jack tonight to the party and tell him this, "When I was sleeping this morning, I think Anson said he detected a leak in the plumbing behind the toilet."

No one had to tell Andie anything twice when it came to her job. She knew immediately that if Jack Gibbens were to be called from the house phone, they were distinctly reminded about some household emergency be mentioned should his presence be requested.

What she didn't know, was just how close to the truth that really was. For two weeks, Anson had been tracking John Smithe's every move. His notes were meticulous. Everything was pretty much routine with one exception.

Last Friday, he left his office with some papers and went into the restroom. Now, that is not very unusual, is it? However, the closest restroom is almost adjacent from his office. On his walk, he passed two employee restrooms and went straight down stairs to the one used by the janitors near the cleaning supply closets.

Anson had been tracking his moves this morning and they were identical to that of last Friday. He got some coffee, Xeroxed a few things, sat down and did some paper work, then promptly spilled the coffee on his pants. It happened again today and if Anson hurried, he somehow knew that he could beat John to that restroom and hide in the stall.

Anson ran down the East corridor, shot down the stairs two flights and entered the floor with the restroom in question. Upon trying the door, he found that it was locked. It was a simple lock that luckily, he had been trained to pick. He worked furiously and then, CLICK – he was in.

Reaching into his pocket, Anson withdrew a note pad that had adhesive on the back. He quickly scrawled "Out of Order" on the note and slapped it onto the stall door. Then he lifted the seat within the stall and stood on it. *Drats! It wasn't good enough. There was too much light. Anyone could see through the cracks, much less a trained Soviet Spy,* he thought. He reached up and grasped the hot lightbulb and unscrewed it just enough to go out. *Ah! Better!* He crouched and waited for the approaching footsteps to make their crucial move.

A key turned in the lock. John Smithe opened the door and turned on the water. He grabbed some soap and started cleaning his pants. It took some time to get the stain out, but Anson was confident that his hunch would play out.

He patiently waiting, noiselessly crouching on the cold porcelain, his thighs were painfully aching from all the running with Andie. Suddenly, the thought of pain withdrew itself from his mind as the scene unfolded before his eyes through the darkened crack and got a lot more fascinating.

John leaned up against the wall and took off his shoe. Turning it over, he released a spring loaded trap door within the heel of the large wing tip shoe.

Of Course! That's perfect. They would never suspect it there and it is virtually undetectable. The metal detector that the employees pass through only covers down to their ankles and might detect the spring in the shoe if it went to the floor!

John gently, as if it were a bomb, took out a tiny rectangular drive. Anson knew immediately what it was. It was the newest thorn in the heart of America. A state of the art camera which could take the picture and instantly process the film into a microdot. When the picture was ejected from the device, it was in the form of one of two things, either a tiny circular band aid, or a thin, clear circular plastic disc that when placed onto black vinyl or leather was virtually undetectable.

Anson could not see which type of film had been ejected, for John had turned his back and began to photograph the blueprints that he had brought with him. Then, with his back still turned from Anson, ejected the tiny rectangle and slipped it into his pocket.

Anson searched his own computer banks in his mind to analyze the data that he had just received. Yes, he had seen John with a tiny band aid on his hand, but he also had a black vinyl briefcase. He couldn't just have him arrested and have the Security Guards pull off a real band aid from a real cut. He had to be sure! He was really groping for straws now.

John left the restroom just as quietly as he had come. Anson waited for about 30 seconds and went directly to the elevator. When he returned to the main office area near Contracts and Negotiations, he stopped near the drinking fountain and got a drink.

Anson looked up as he tried to quench his thirst for a clue. Just as John reached into his shirt pocket and took out the tiny piece of paper, a large hulking shadow appeared right in Anson's line of vision!

"Anson! Hey! I'm excited about tonight. My wife wanted to know if she could bring an hors d'oeuvre that she's been dying to try out on someone," Bruiser grinned.

"That's great, Bruiser," Anson said halfheartedly. Gingerly stretching his lanky frame, he peeked around Bruiser's massive shoulder to see John setting his case down on the floor and then he just happened to touch the band aid.

"Anything. She can bring anything she wants," he patted Bruiser on the back as he left the area.

DARN! I was so close! All I had to do is see where he placed it and then I could have made a solid arrest! This is going to take longer than I thought!

The ride home was pretty quiet. Anson told John that he was tired. He wasn't really looking forward to hosting this stupid party that Andie had schemed up. Anson took a little longer getting out of the car than usual.

"Sore muscles, John," he explained. "Adie has me on this running kick that's going to kill me. I just want to go out and do a little light jogging, but nooooo," he complained.

"Hey, at least you're getting exercise. Maybe I'll start up with you guys. What time do you go?" he asked.

"About five. Roosters aren't even up at 5, but we are," Anson whined.

"I don't think I could cut that any more. That sounds like when we were in the Military. I sometimes work late re-writing contracts. We'll have to find something else? Golf?" he asked.

Anson was so excited about having a golf partner, that he didn't really notice that Eve, the housekeeper had come out and taken John's coat and briefcase to the house.

Suddenly, the dawn of reality touched a memory in the fog within his brain. This epiphany was a surprising realization that he was looking for.

Didn't she do that one-day last week? Friday. It WAS Friday. That is the same day he poured coffee on himself. She must be tied in with this thing somehow.

Waving good-bye, Anson invited John to bring Emily over and meet some of their friends at a little get together they were going to have.

As soon as John went inside, Anson raced home to tell Andie what he found out. Little did he know, she had done some investigating this afternoon on her own and already knew.

13 An Epiphany

Andie opened the front door shortly after calling Jack to invite him. On the way to the wailing door bell, she made jokes.

Wow Jack. That's service. I give you a call and instantly, you appear at my door. Do you have a phone in your shoe?

Opening the door, she found little Faith in tears. Quickly, she invited her in and tried to console her.

"What is it? What's the matter, dear? Please come in," she drew her arms around her.

"That stupid Eve or Anna, whatever her name is. She hates me. I tell you, she hates me!" she cried.

Whatever are you talking about? The maid? The grouchy maid with the blond hair? Maybe it's because she's secretly bald under that wig? Faith, did she hurt you?" she snarled her lip.

It worked. Faith was giggling through her tears. Andie took it a step farther.

"Maybe she takes out her teeth at night. That's the only date she has!" Andie roared.

Faith was laughing so much; she fell onto the couch.

"Does she walk like this and carry a whip?" she imitated the Hunchback of Notre dame. The little girl clutched her stomach and hollered for her to halt the cornball routine.

"Stop. I'll have to go to the bathroom," she tried to catch her breath, then they collapsed together in each other's arms giggling at the thought of what Andie had contrived.

"Oh Andie. I love you! You make me laugh. I just wanted a cookie. It's not too close to dinner, really. She grabbed my hand so tight, look!" she thrust her hand forth to Andie for inspection. "and called me a name that I've never heard of. It was in some weird language," she sighed.

"Weird language, huh? Maybe she is from outer space. Does she sound like an alien? Here, I've got lots of goodies. Remember? I bought half the store last time I was there. Let's change Eve into a princess. Come on!" she jogged to the kitchen with Faith in tow.

"A princess? Yes, she is an alien. She says, "boars what pigs," all the time. Hey, Are you a witch? Only a witch could change her!" she shouted.

"No, a writer. I can create magic, Faith. Have some Faith!" she laughed as she pulled out all kinds of junk food out of the pantry. Running to the cupboard, she got out a couple of glasses and poured some juice from the refrigerator. Then, they sat down to the computer. *What did boars and pigs have in common*, Andie wondered.

"First tell me everything about Eve. I'll write down what she is really like, then we will change her name and hair and eyes to different colors and make her a happy princess instead of a grouchy Cinderella. Sound like fun?" she asked.

Faith nodded eagerly. They already had the first part. Her name and her blonde hair.

"Okay, what color are her eyes?" Andie asked.

"Well, one is brown and the other is blue," Faith answered.

"What?" Andie was puzzled.

"Well, one night, I woke up and went downstairs to get a drink. I forgot to knock. It was an accident. I walked into her bathroom and her wig was in the sink. She had one blue eye and one brown eye. She got so mad at me, she pushed me against the door and talked in angry alien. She hurt my arm.," she answered timidly.

"She does sound like a witch," Andie was on to something. Contact lenses!

"What happened next?" Andie was curious.

"Well, she started screaming at me and her hair fell down," she said.

Andie gasped, "You mean she really was bald?" she teased.

"No, she has lovely dark hair. She was trying to wrap it into a bun, but when I came in, it all came apart and she came unglued!" Faith said.

"She didn't hit you, did she?" Andie was leading her.

"Yes! That's when Daddy came rushing in and tried to make her feel better and be more quiet. He didn't even look at my arm. That's when he called her "Ah ha!" she said dramatically with her arm draped across her forehead.

"Ok, so the next day, when she had her blonde wig on again, did she have her other brown eye on?" she tested.

"No," she answered. "I looked too! She always had blue eyes when she has the wig on."

"Well, eat up. Let's turn her into a princess for real," and she wrote a little story. She couldn't let her have a print out to take home. That would have blown her cover if Anna would have found it.

"Let's see. What shall we name her? Eve? Anna? Eve? Anna?" Andie's eyes grew as large as saucers as she leapt up from the computer. Suddenly Andie had a big epiphany!

Ivana! Not Ivan Doblinsky. Ivana Doblinsky is living right across the street from me. My gosh. Right under my nose. Boars and pigs.... bourgeoisie pigs – that's a comment insulting the upper class of Americans. I've got to get upstairs and scan those hard copies.

"Faith, whenever you come over we'll write another princess episode, but let's change her name to Hope. She will be your imaginary sister, alright?" Andie asked as she walked Faith to the door.

"Okay, Andie!" she gave her a hug. "Thank you for making me feel better," she smiled as she left.

Andie raced upstairs and groped through hundreds of pictures until she found one of a woman leaving in the dark with a scarf and glasses. She hadn't given it much thought until now. It was last Friday. She wanted to call Anson at work, but he was on his way home

14 Utter gossip?

Anson now got out of John's car and raced across the street as soon as John had gone into the house. He fought every muscle in his body in doing so. He was so excited that the adrenaline propelled him into the door. Andie, in her excitement opened the door to greet Anson with her news. Unfortunately, Anson's judgement was off and went sliding across the entry way floor that Bess had just waxed.

Tumbling into the corner, he hit a table holding a large ceramic vase filled with pampas grass stalks. The white plumes began to fly and the vase started tumbling through the air. Andie leaped and caught the vase, rolling over onto her back to cushion the blow, she too slid over the freshly waxed marble floor.

"Oh! I got it!" she screamed as she slid right into Anson's arms with the vase.

"Nice work, Ace," he laughed helping her to her feet.

Both were talking AT each other as fast as they could. Neither one was listening to their stories of the day. It was the first real break in two weeks, and it was a good one.

"Maid? Did you say maid? How could you know about that?" Anson faced the enigma cautiously.

"Housekeeper? You mean Anna? Anson, it's really Ivana Doblinsky, not Ivan. No wonder the Bureau has never seen her. They are looking for a man, not a woman," Andie told him the rest of the story that she had learned during her investigation.

"This is bigger than the both of us. We've got to get Jack over here right away," Anson decided going over to the phone.

"Done. He should be here shortly. We're meeting in the Castle's cottage. There's his car now and the Caterers just pulled up behind him. Let me get them under control and then we'll talk," she excused herself.

Inez Caruso was equally as perturbed to be called away from an important dinner engagement with a client. She voiced her opinion to Jack as she met him on the walkway.

"This had better be good, Jack. If these rookies, fresh off the farm, are going to be calling us every few minutes to tell us utter gossip, this job is going to be a royal pain in the neck and a cramp in my style," she shook her finger vehemently in his face.

"Hey, Inez, chill out. You were young once too, you know. Hey, I know it's still early in the investigation, but you never know, they could have run across a fluke. Let's let them play their hand. You know, give them wisdom and guidance like us old fogies are supposed to, then we will play cleanup batter and sew this thing up. Look, they've still got all the quick moves, but we've got the smarts. Now be a good dame, and ring the doorbell. We're being chased by caterers."

"For you, Jack. Only for you," Inez grumbled, "but....it better be good."

When Andie opened the door, Jack and Inez stepped into the entry way only to find a mess of pampas grass still flying upwards in a flurry as each little draft caught a tuft.

"My dear, what have you done? These things are only rented!" Inez exclaimed.

"It was only an accident, Ms. Caruso, and we SAVED the vase! Now if you will all follow me, we'll go out to the Castle's bungalow," she smiled charmingly and led the team.

Harry and Bess paced furiously as they waited for the others to arrive. Looking at their guests walking towards the bungalow from the pool area, Bess sighed.

"What do you think it is, Harry?" she asked

"I think they found out something big and this is going to end sooner than we expected. Gee does that mean we'll get less money? Let's hope it doesn't get messy. I cleaned my gun today. I'm ready, are you?" Harry tested her strength.

"Harry Castle, you clean that gun twice every day. Yes, I guess I'm ready. I counted on assisting on the surveillance work, because I'm not combat ready, Harry. And you aren't either, dear. Your reactions can't possibly hold a candle to those kids and they certainly can't be what they were thirty years ago. You're an old fool to think you can out shoot these new Agents. Why, the technology in weaponry is so far advanced that you'd be lying there pushing up daisies before they said, "Freeze," she huffed.

"Bess, I can do this. I can do whatever they tell me. No, I can judge for myself and do whatever the situation calls for," his confidence was building.

"Harry, what if...I mean, we never discussed the possibility of one of us not making it," Bess pouted. Harry squeezed her hand as the doorbell rang.

Anson was the first to arrive. He shook Harry and Bess' hands and then waited anxiously for the others. When all were seated, Anson described the activities that had taken place in the bathroom at work.

"First of all, Jack, I need one of those cameras that Smithe was using. I'm convinced that he is using the kind with a clear, pliable adhesive dot backing. He's sticking it onto the corner of his briefcase, I'm sure. When he is out to lunch Monday, I'm going to check for residues on the case. That way, I'll know exactly where to place the duplicate. I'll also need a briefcase that is identical to his. I'm going to take a few picture of my own and switch cases with him," he rubbed his chin.

"That's good. Switch cases, then switch the dots. When he realizes that you've got the wrong case, you won't have much time, you know," Jack noted.

"I've got that covered. After the switch, I'll go directly into the lab. He won't be able to follow me in there. I'll merely discover the accident and return it to him," Jack said.

"Ok, then what?" asked Harry.

"We come over here and wait for Ivana to leave. At that point Smithe will be out of it and we can pick him up later," Inez assumed.

"Has she information to turn over to her contacts tonight?" Bess wanted to know.

"That's the information that you caught him photographing today, correct?" Andie questioned.

"Yes, but I can't concern myself with dummy information being passed. He knows all of you – you'd be spotted," said Anson.

"Inez nodded. "Yes, your cover could be blown before we pass what they have been waiting for."

"Exactly. Let's give Smithe some serious bait to sink his teeth into. Do you think Dr. Brennery could have her people work up some phony information and blueprints before next Friday?" asked Jack

"It would take some doing, but O'Rourke wants this thing stopped. I think he will cooperate," Anson said.

"Okay, then that's the plan. You set it up at work. We'll be ready to go, next Friday night. Plan to be here at 5:00. Inez and I can't very well tail them in a Century 21 car or a Pink Cadillac with Inez Interiors plastered all over the sides, so we'll ride with you. Harry and Bess, follow as back up. Anything else Anson?" Jack didn't want to take total control.

"No, that just about covers it. If we can do this, we'll probably get medals! Jack, you need to let the Director of Operations know that we've got Ivana Doblinsky surrounded and the situation is pretty much in our control now," Anson advised.

"I don't know about the rest of you, but I'm starved. There's a party about to arrive and a mess to be cleaned up in the entry way. The Smithes have been invited tonight. Do you want us to introduce you as casual friends?" Andie asked.

They all nodded and Bess offered to help Andie in the house. Before long, the guests were arriving and enjoying the music that Andie had put on.

15 A Little Counseling

"Where did you get that music, Andie?" Anson asked quietly. "It's a nice touch," he added.

"Remember, I'm a Writer. Writers hang out at book stores. I happened to find a Church book store! They've got tons of music there. When this is all done, I'll probably write a book about Mormon terminology, trust me, it's a needed resource.," she whispered.

Vaughn and Annette stepped through the doorway with a plate of hot and spicy chicken wings in her arms. Her beaming face suddenly fell.

"Vaughn, how could you?" she hissed.

"What? How could I what? What did I do wrong?" he forced a smile through his whisper so none would be the wiser.

With her eyes darting back and forth around the room, she quickly surveyed the situation and rolled her eyes in his direction, feeling like diving under the couch.

"This is a catered affair. You don't bring food to a catered event, Vaughn. How could you get the information so boggled up? I kid you not, if it doesn't have anything to do with football or airplanes, you just can't seem to get the facts straight," she whispered back, exuding the same fake smile.

Bruiser sheepishly hung his head and tried to make her smile. "I'm sorry, honey. Can you forgive me?" he asked.

Suddenly Anson spying the situation from across the room realized in a second what had happened. Quickly like a good wing man, he went to Bruiser's aid.

"Annette. You've saved the party! Bruiser told me what a great cook you are. If you hadn't brought these, I would have been stuck eating fish eggs and liver squiggles all night. How can I ever thank you?" he asked, giving her a hug and taking the plate.

"Well, since you put it that way, you just go on now and enjoy them. Vaughn, sweetie, do you really like the way I cook?" she asked as her eyes sparkled up to the towering figure above her.

"Of course, dear. You're the greatest!" he grinned and thanked Anson with a wink for saving his fuselage once more.

"Anson dear, is there somewhere I could put my jacket?" she asked.

"Sure, Annette. Right upstairs in the Master bedroom. Just make yourself at home," Anson grinned.

Annette climbed the stairs and opened the door. He hadn't really said which door was the Master Bedroom, so she decided to try them all so that she could figure it out. *Ok that was the easy way to be nosey.* Logically, the first room was decorated in browns and there were mostly "men" types of things around.

Everything was perfectly in place and extremely orderly. The second was a large spacious room. It was sparsely decorated and nothing was out of place. If she had to pick, this would definitely be the Master Bedroom. On either side of the room was a huge walk in closet and spa bathrooms. There was something missing that Annette just could not put her finger on. She decided to try the next door just in case it was bigger than this one.

When she opened it, the room looked like a disaster. It looked like the room of a teenager, but she knew they had no children. The items that she saw were typically female in nature by the clothes that dotted the floor. It all seemed highly unusual, but she brushed it off and went back to the largest room.

Not wanting to miss another moment of the party, Annette went over to the closet to get a hanger for her coat. The bedspread certainly looked too new and nice to lay anything on it. When she opened the closet she became completely befuddled. The closet was completely bare.

Ok, she thought to herself. *So they don't have a lot of clothes and share a closet. I'll check his for a hanger.* When she did, again, she found nothing. She curiously went into the Master Bathroom on the female side and opened a few drawers. Again nothing. Now she realized what was wrong with the room. Not that it wasn't nice to have neat, clean surroundings, but there were no personal adornments hanging around; no wedding pictures, no engagement pictures.   Certainly nothing of College memorabilia. It seemed so odd and then she realized that perhaps they did not inhabit the marital room at all.

They have separate bedrooms. They don't even sleep together. Their marriage must be in trouble. I've got to tell Vaughn.   Maybe there's something he can do to help. That's it. They just need a little counseling, that's all!

Vaughn, in the meantime had come upstairs in search of Annette.   Not knowing what room to check in, he accidentally opened the surveillance room which Harry had left unlocked while he went downstairs for a soda and some cookies.

Vaughn looked around the room and knew immediately it was not the normal hobby room in a home. It looked like an arsenal of military grade weapons and high tech peep equipment for communications. This looked a lot more serious than some of the com rooms he had witnessed at Top Gun and out in the field.   He sensed he should not be there and hurriedly backed out of the room.

At the same time, Annette was backing slowly out of the Master Bedroom and they bumped behinds as they closed the doors. Both gasped in surprise and fear as a little child would, had he been caught with his fingers in the cookie jar. Red faced and adrenaline flowing, they embraced and went downstairs, not wanting to tell the other what they had each found.

"Here comes Bishop Elliot. Look, he's got Faith with him," Anson said.

"Do you two know each other?" Andie asked.

"Yes, this is my friend's father. Do you remember me talking about Sandy?" Faith beamed.

"Anson, could you and I have a word together?" the Bishop asked quietly.

"Sure. Come into the library," Anson followed him.

"This really isn't the place to discuss this," the bishop said, looking at the extensive library on Mormon Heritage. "Say, this is the most complete personal library that I have ever seen. How long have you been collecting these?" he wondered.

"Uh, I don't really remember. It seems like years," he fumbled.

"Uh. Huh. Anson, I'm in an awkward position. Your records still haven't been found from your last Ward. When I called that Ward, they don't seem to remember you," he paused. You see, there's this little girlfriend of my daughter's wo wants to join the church. It seems like you've made a great impression upon her and she wants to be baptized."

"You mean Faith? Faith wants to be a member of the Church?" Anson seemed surprised.

"Not only that, she only wants **you** to baptize her. Since I don't really know your status, I'm not sure how to answer her. Do you see my position?" he asked.

"Status?" Anson asked slowly.

"Yes. You're not making this easy for me, are you? I guess I just need to know if you are a worthy member in good standing," asked the Bishop as gently as he could.

"Do I have to answer this now?" Anson twiddled his fingers in his lap.

"Son, this isn't a trick question. Hmm. I would really like you and your wife to meet with me on Sunday after Church. There's some things that we just have to get to the bottom of. I'm sure I can help you both," smiled the Bishop.

"Sir, there's just one thing. Can a person. not anyone we know mind you, be put in jail for impersonating a Mormon?" he smiled weakly.

"I don't think so. Son, I'm not sure that I can work major miracles. Being a man of great faith, I can do many things. However, that kind of problem, I am sure, I could fix," the Bishop laughed as he shook his hand.

While Anson was out of the room with the Bishop, Jack Gibbens took a sip from his punch and looked around. When he was certain that no one was looking, he slipped upstairs to the surveillance room. Taking out a walkie talkie, he spoke to someone in the distance and then slipped out again.

As the Bishop got into his car to leave, some of the other guests were laughing as they left the driveway. No one from the party, especially Andie or Anson, seemed to notice the young woman with a scarf and glasses leave the neighbor's house in her car. In addition, in the haste to leave the neighborhood, an additional car appeared to be leaving. The shadowy figure lurking behind the wheel, honed in on the young woman's car and followed her every move.

16 The Belle Star

Friday – July 27, 1990 – 21:00 hours – Offshore Malibu Beach

The Belle Star, steamed along the sea lanes that follow the California coastline. The huge tanker made her way North as she stopped occasionally and drank from the derricks that dotted the coastal waters. With each meal, she lumbered on, a little slower and a little lower in the water.

Her home port was out of San Diego. Working for two major oil companies, she knew which derricks to visit on her North bound route, dumping her precious load in San Francisco. Occasionally, she made it up to Alaska to grab a load and deliver it to the Bay Area. Turning around, she would begin her route again. That time, she would head Southward. Light, and at a quicker pace, she would again drink from different derricks and relinquish her heavy burden back in San Diego to another Oil Company.

To protect herself from stubbing a toe on the bottom of the ocean, and losing her precious life blood to the depths of the sea, she was well equipped with sonar. It seemed to work perfectly until recently.

Coxswain's mate, Sam Deer jiggled the connection on the sonar reading device.

"Captain there it goes again. I know these waters. We are supposed to be at 150 fathoms. The reading keeps telling me 140. It's almost as if we gained 60 feet of hull," he complained.

The captain sauntered over to the machine. He knows the capabilities of his ship, as a good captain should. He also knows that something isn't right. *Surely the ocean floor hadn't shifted this much in a week*, he thought.

"Right rudder, 30 degrees, all engines full," he bellowed and his demands were echoed by the other members of his crew.

"Let's take her closer and see if we get the same readings as we head into shallow waters," he continued watching with his eyes glued to the monitor.

"No change, sir," Sam spoke

"Left rudder, 60 degrees, all engines full!" the Captain bellowed once more.

"We're still 10 to 15 fathoms off no matter what course we take," the Coxswain advised.

"Hmmm. I see. Well, this far out, knowing the waters as well as we do, I can't see what, if any discrepancy like could do us any harm, but when we get closer to the Bay Area, we'll have to be escorted. I'll not hang this lady up on a sand barge. When we get past Carmel, notify the Coast Guard to stand by. For now, disregard any further mis readings," he spoke firmly.

"Aye, Aye, Captain," he said.

Point Mugu – Naval Air Station – Air/Sea Traffic Control Center 22:00 hours

"Ensign Adams, reporting for duty, sir," the young man slapped to attention.

"At ease, Ensign. So, you've been relieved of air traffic duty, hmmm? Too tough for you? Don't worry. It takes a certain breed of animal to be able to deal with that kind of stress. Those birds travel at a pretty high speed. The reaction time is very critical," he spoke uncritically at first.

"Yes, sir," the Ensign looked straight ahead.

"Relax, Ensign. You're used to looking at screens. This is your scope, right here. Here's our book of fish. I want you to memorize every sub, carrier, destroyer and rowboat in the whole United States Navy. Then we'll start on the Soviet Fish, Chinese, etc., Got me?" the Commander eyed him critically.

"Yes, sir, Commander sir!" he shouted.

"Ensign. I said relax," the Commander sneered sarcastically. "Like I said, we don't have much quick action deployment around here, but we do like to be accurate when we do so. You need to be precise, exact, no wavering, and no second opinions, got the picture?" he smiled through the side of his mouth.

"Yes, sir!" the Ensign refused to look at the Commander as a good sailor is trained to. He had been warned about the Ax-man, and he wasn't about to screw this job up.

Commander Ray Waxman, had served valiantly in Vietnam then did a stint at Top Gun, but his first love was here, now training the future Commanders of the United States Navy, that is, if they could cut it.

After hearing about the Ensign's screw up when he almost put two F-18s in the drink during a routine landing on a carrier, he was going to watch this boy very closely.

"We get a lot of tankers, fishing vessels and sailboats around here. Just a few little things to cut your teeth on," he said as he shoved the remaining sonar books into the Ensign's hand.

"As you were," he stormed out. The Ensign sat down to the screen and stared into its vast blue color. Little moving non-descript blips appeared here and there. As he watched them float slowly across the screen, determined to succeed, he opened the first book and began to devour the material and commit it to memory.

Being new to the program, he did not see the shadowy figure depart from the starboard side of the tanker blip on the screen and turn eastward toward the Coast. Nor did he know, that lying now, less than one mile from the Coast off

Malibu, was a fully armed Victor Class 2 Soviet Submarine ready to surface and deploy a raft to the shoreline.

17 Darn that Jargon

Sunday morning, Andie and Anson went to Church with determination to confess all to the Bishop. Even though they were at a critical point in the investigation, they both felt confident that he would guide them just as the Director would guide them on tactical issues of the Operation.

During Sacrament, they held hands, for appearance sake, or was it? Anson kept looking down at Andie's shiny hair. She would feel his gaze, look up and smile. There was something when their eyes met that read more than just duty to their job.

During Sunday School, they both answered questions about 3ʳᵈ Nephi in such an excited manner that the old line Mormons, having heard it all their lives woke up and took notice.

"As I read 3 Nephi, Chapter 18, Verse 20, my testimony of the Gospel of Jesus Christ is strengthened. I know without a shadow of a doubt that this Church is true. I feel like telling the whole world about it! Just listen to this:

20   And whatsoever ye shall ask the Father in my name, which is light, believing that ye shall receive, behold it shall be given unto you.

21   Pray in your families unto the Father, always my name, that your wives and your children may be blessed.

After I read that, I did pray. I prayed like I've never prayed before, and I had great faith that Heavenly Father would tell me exactly what to do. I know now that I was supposed to be a member of this Church all my life.," he spoke with conviction and emotion brimming in his throat and thought *I know what I have to do.*

Andie's eyes brimmed with tears as she looked up at Anson. She was so proud of him and her heart was so full of...love?

What am I feeling for him? Is this love? Could it be love? I prayed too. I asked for a sign that continuing to come to the Church was what I needed to do. This must be it. Oh, Anson! I do love you!

When Anson sat down, he was shaking. The rest of the Sunday School class was moved also. Others began sharing their testimonies of praying for faith, and answers to their questions. They knew that Heavenly Father heard their prayers, but Anson and Andie could not hear them. They were staring at each other with new eyes and telling each other their secret thoughts through their smiles.

"Meet me outside the Bishop's office," Anson whispered.

I'll be there," she whispered back, her lips brushing his ear.

After church, Andie sat in one of the two chairs on one side of the door. She waited patiently for Anson to arrive from his Priesthood lesson. On the other side of the door, were two young men in suits. They had name tags on. Each bore the first name of Elder.

"Are you...missionaries?" she asked.

They looked at each other and smiled. "Yes, we are," one said.

"Where are you from?" she wondered.

"Well, I'm from Idaho and my partner is from Utah," he smiled.

"Your first names," she paused, starring at the name badges. "Both Elder. Is that unusual?" she asked.

"Do a lot of Mormon mothers name their sons Elder? I mean, you've got to admit, coming from two different states and getting a companion with the same first name, that seems like there must be a lot of Elders in the world," she asked innocently.

"The two Elders, thought she was joking and began to laugh.

"That's one for the book, eh Elder Smith?" one laughed.

"I've got to remember to write that one to my Mom, Elder Webb. That will make her smile," he laughed.

Andie wasn't laughing. She couldn't really figure out how she had done it, but she was pretty sure that she had made another error in Mormon jargons. She gracefully laughed along with the Elders. The Bishop and Anson arrived just in time to bail her out of the potentially embarrassing mess.

The Bishop invited them in and opened with prayer. This time, Anson asked to give it. He had read a pamphlet outside the Bishop's office on his last visit that taught the proper way to pray, and executed the task eloquently.

In his prayer, he asked that the Bishop listen with understanding to their problem, and knowing all that he had studied and prayed about, he had great faith that this would be so.

When he was done, Anson asked, "Bishop, you are a smart man, please tell me what it is that you have already surmised from our situation," he smiled.

The Bishop sat up in his chair and folded his hands on the desk.

"I know that you are two fine and decent people. I know that somehow you have been brought to our Church and yet you have found the truth on your own. I also know that you have never been baptized, served a mission or been to the Temple, so I must also assume, that you are living together unmarried. I don't know exactly how far your relationship has progressed, but I can tell that you both love each other very much. How am I doing," he paused.

"I'd say six for six, sir. We never meant to deceive you. It was a matter of national security," he smiled.

"Now, I've got to admit. That's one I've never heard of before. Not only have I never had anyone pretend to be Mormons, but to claim to be protecting their Country in doing so! Do tell more, this fascinates me! You have my attention," he smiled.

"We're FBI agents. Our assignment was to infiltrate the community and blend in with your Religion as a cover so that we would not be recognized as a threat to Russian agents while trying to uncover a spy ring. We are almost at the end of our assignment. If all goes well, in a week or so, our work will be finished, but I think that I speak for both of us when I say it can't end there. I, we, want it all. We want to be baptized, and we want....," he paused and looked down at Andie.

She looked at him with adoring eyes and encouraged him to go on. She squeezed his hand and made him say the words.

"...to be married. Right away, I think. We haven't done anything bad or anything like that," he spoke quickly. "By the way, how did you know so much?"

The Bishop smiled. The situation wasn't at all as bad as he had first imagined. This was something he could certainly remedy.

"A Bishop has many sources. When you didn't know what a calling was, or a Temple recommend, I thought that maybe you had been excommunicated. When your records ceased to exist I became more curious. Your library was more extensive than any member that I have ever met, and all new books, too. A few well-meaning guests at your party wandered where they shouldn't have and confided in me their worst fears. It took a lot to keep them quiet. But the most interesting source of all was little Faith, my daughter's friend, who loves to talk. Need I say more?" he laughed.

"No! Can you help us?" they wanted to know.

"First, yes, you can be baptized immediately. The second may be a little more difficult depending on the sensitivity of the situation. My sources tell me that you are living in separate rooms. Does that mean that you are both morally clean?" he gently asked.

They both looked at each other and giggled. They knew exactly what he meant.

"Yes. We have a married couple as chaperones and locks on our doors. Does that answer your questions?" the smiled.

"I don't suppose that you could wait a year and be married in the Temple first?" he wondered.

"Is that usually how it's done?" Andie Asked. Anson frowned, not wanting to wait any longer.

"It is best to seal your marriage for time and all eternity under the roof of the Temple, but in this particular case, we could marry you here, then in one year, you can be sealed there. You'll need a license. It will take three days. Do I have your word that you two will behave yourselves until then?" he grinned.

"We've lasted this long. I'm sure it will be something to look forward to," Anson promised. Andie nodded in accordance.

"In that case, let me introduce you to my own Secret Agents," he said as he opened the door.

He invited the Missionaries in and briefed them on the secrecy of the matter. They would hold the baptism in the evening when everyone had gone home, this would accomplish the first task, and thus keep the Ward from spreading undue questions and gossip.

Then, for step two, he invited them to return to his office the following Sunday, assuming their case would be closed, and he would perform the marriage ceremony in his office.

There was one other matter the Bishop was concerned with.

"Everything you have told me will be kept in complete confidence, but your old friend Vaughn, is my counselor. He doesn't really need to know any of this until you tell him, but if you would allow me to do so, I promise you that he would be discreet. He has spent the last two nights completely sleepless as he is filled with worry, confusion and compassion for you."

"Will he tell his wife? She's a doll, but I can't take the chance...," Anson began.

"Anything told to a Bishop or his Counselor is kept in strictest confidence. With your permission, the only thing that she will be told is that you are both receiving the proper counseling and that soon everything will be wonderful," he suggested.

"It's a deal," he said.

They closed with a prayer and went their separate ways until that evening. Anson was baptized and confirmed, then the Bishop baptized Andie in the waters within the Ward building. Now they were both confirmed members of The Church of Jesus Christ of Latter Day Saints.

When they returned home, they were holding hands and dreamy eyed under the moonlight. They continued to make grand plans about where they wanted their FBI base to be after the case was solved. They both had different ideas on what type of place they would rent. They agreed that they certainly could not afford to live in this house even on their combined salaries.

As they opened the door, they were surprised to find Jack Gibbens waiting on the living room couch.

"It took a lot of strings, but I finally found one. Here's the camera that you wanted. Do you know that it had to be flown here from Washington D.C? We also got the film that you wanted. Those Japanese sure know how to build cameras! I know you wanted one that was a Polaroid, but Polaroid doesn't make this type of camera. So Polaroid has the distinct properties to instantly develop a picture. This one takes it one step further. It uses that type of technology, but it does output onto microdots. Amazing isn't it?

Here's the briefcase. Luckily, the security guard has been keeping an eye on Smithe for so long, he practically memorized every nick and scratch. I hope this works. I had to get some pretty important people out of bed to accomplish it over the last two days. They are really pulling for you guys," he said.

"Jack, I knew I could count on you. You seem to have connections all over the USA," Anson grinned.

"Just keep your head down. Maybe we'll work together again, eh? Listen, call me if there's any changes of plans, otherwise...Friday at 5:00 pm, he clicked his fingers as he walked out the door.

Anson walked Andie to her room and kissed her goodnight.

"I love you Andie even though you can't cook, you don't like to pick up your clothes and you could probably beat me up if you wanted to," he said lovingly. "You don't know what a step that is for me," he added.

"And I love you Anson even though you're overly neat, can't pick out your own clothes, worry too much about things that probably won't happen and we can eat out sometimes," she touched his chin with her index finger.

"Lock your door," he said as he walked away.

18 Upside down!

Monday morning would come soon enough for Anson. He tossed and turned all night as he went over the plans for the day in his mind. First and foremost, he had to act perfectly natural with John Smithe as he drove both of them to work.

Secondly, he had to speak to Mr. O'Rourke and Dr. Brennery as soon as he arrived. It would take time for implementation of the plan in order for things to run smoothly. Could Joan fake a systems analysis report that, at a glance could fool John? Would it be possible for Mike to put John in charge of the seemingly sensitive information?

All these questions and more buzzed in his mind while he was shaving, dressing and driving to work. There was one thought that left a lump in his throat.

Could little Faith, who wished that I baptize her, ever forgive me once she finds out that I helped put her father in prison for treason?

If the Government chooses to execute John for his efforts in unleashing top secret information, will she ever be able to hold onto her faith in God?

She would, Anson knew, eventually find out that he was working against her Dad, but how could an eight-year-old child be made to see that duty to God and Country were far more precious, but what price is Country over love for a parent.

As he pulled into the Northrup compound, he tried to keep his mind from clouding as he discussed plans for a golf game with John.

I've got to remember that the first thing they taught me was not to get personally involved. It's so hard, but it's got to be done. Besides, Andie thinks John or that babysitter might be abusing Faith; won't do to get too chummy.

Anson walked up to Mike O'Rourke's office. He started to knock on the door but an elderly, bespectacled woman with a stern look on her face stopped him. Tottering upon high heels to make her appear taller, she reached up and tapped him viciously on the shoulder.

"Young man," she snapped. You have no appointment! You can't just go barging in on Mr. O'Rourke without an appointment," she continued. She was so upset and agitated that a strand of gray hair came loose from her bun.

"But, Mike told me that anytime I wanted to talk to him, I could just come on up. It's important. I wouldn't bother him if it weren't: he insisted.

"That's what they all say," she hissed as she pinched his arm and walked him towards the door. "Now you just come away from that door, or I'll have to call Security!"

"No. Take your hands off me, please. I've got to talk to Mr. O'Rourke. It's URGENT!" he explained. With that, he wrenched himself free of her spider like grip and stood away from her.

"Now then. No one takes that tone of voice with me! I'll just have your job for that!" She began to dial Security when Mike's door opened slowly and he appeared shaking his head and smiling.

"Now, now, Miss Van Briggle. Everything's fine. I should have told you about Mr. Wellings, here. It's my fault, Alice, really. Now Anson won't you come in?" she smiled.

"REALLY, Mr. O'Rourke?" she smiled sweetly. "I'm only trying to do my job. I can't let just any riff-raff come knocking at your door without an appointment, you know.," she said a little snootily.

"Right you are Alice. But now, remember, those people usually stay with Joe down at the main gate. I'm grateful for your diligence, however, I wouldn't mind a gentler touch, hmm?" he smiled.

When they were safely inside, he set the controls for the music on the intercom loud enough to scramble any attempts at overhearing their conversation. Then, he mentioned for Anson to stand near the speakers as they talked quietly.

Anson explained the situation that had occurred on Friday and the plan that lay ahead of them. He asked for Mike's assistance in carrying it off.

"Do you think you can swing this, Mike? You've got to give him clearance to work on the plans, but not until about Thursday. Do you need another week, or can Joan devise something close to the most recent version of the specs for the Stealth 2 by then?" he asked.

"Close? We've been close for six years. We've been working on this long before we were ever given the go ahead for the bid. We've got so many CLOSE plans; it could fill the lab with paperwork. She'll have no problem there. As for the other problem, I think that I can grant him clearance without arousing suspicion. There was a time once before I cleared him for some last minute work. Hmmm. That won't be a problem. I'll talk to Joan and get the ball rolling," he said.

"Thanks. The sooner we close this case, the sooner we can all move forward," Anson said.

The door opened and in walked Joan, Obviously, she had heard the last sentence or two.

"You'll get Joan rolling on what?" she asked.

"How did you do that? You just walked right by the Wicked Witch of the East. Did you put a spell on her or what?" Anson snickered.

"You have to know how to ease yourself around her, that's all, Wellings," she smiled. "You also have to bring her chocolates once in a while and remember her birthday. Then you get the run of the place," she laughed.

"Oh, I get it. Bribery. Quality security system, Mike! I get it.," he laughed.

"Joan, Anson was just briefing me on the latest findings of our investigation. It seems that when designing the Security System, we should have made it more extensive. Our suspect has been bringing a highly specialized camera into our compound hidden in the heel of his shoe. There's just no way we could have figured for something like that. Our sensors hit him about mid heel to ankle level so one, of course, we'll have to start reconfiguring that, and two, we also need to start looking for microdots on briefcases and purses. We might be able to scan for that with the right equipment. We were right to cooperate with the FBI. This is much more serious than we anticipated," Mike shook his head.

Don't worry, Mike. If Dr. Joan here, can give us a hand, we'll have your criminal behind bars within the week, I'm sure," Anson spoke confidently.

"Ok, you know what you have to do," Anson said as he walked out the door.

Anson spent the rest of the morning going through files in Contracts and Negotiations. Whenever anyone asked him what someone from Research and Development needed in the files, he merely said, "Mr. O'Rourke wants me to familiarize myself with other projects that we've done at this facility in the past."

It seemed to do the trick and gave him time to keep an eye on John. At 10 o'clock, several of the people from the first shift left to go to the cafeteria on their break. John stayed behind. Anson knew that he blew his chance to check his briefcase. In frustration, he passed the area, reading furiously through folders.

Suddenly, it happened. John obviously had some errand to run and was taking his break later. He sat his case on the desk and walked out of the room. As soon as he did, Anson went over and sat down at his desk. He sat his files on top of John's briefcase. Then with his arms fully extended, held onto the briefcase, cradling the papers on top of his arms. Gently as he pretended to read, he checked the case for sticky residues. Nothing.

No, how can this be? I'm sure this is how it's getting out. I'll have to turn it over.

Anson tried to be inconspicuous as he turned the case over. There it was on the upper right hand corner. The sticky residue that he had been trained to find was warm under his fingertips. There wasn't much. It was apparent that John had tried to clean it off, perhaps with alcohol, by the odor he detected.

Before Anson could turn it back over, he saw John coming back down the hall out of the corner of his eye. He sensed that any second John would see him too as he sat at John's desk!

Slowly Anson picked up the papers that he was reading and leaned back in the chair and put his feet up on the desk. It was a casual move that eluded deception.

"Anson?" John's face showed concern. "What are you doing at my desk?"

"John!" Anson smiled as his chair slapped the floor and he almost lost his balance as if surprised. "I got tired of standing up trying to read through all those blue prints and contracts. I saw that you weren't using your desk. I'm sorry. I didn't think you'd mind," Anson said coolly.

"Oh," John's eyebrows slowly became more relaxed and un knit. "Yeah, I guess that's okay. You didn't touch anything, did you?" John asked.

"I don't think so. Just these," Anson got up, gathered his papers and started to walk out of the office. "Oh, I forgot – are we going to get in 18 this Saturday? Can you set it up with the Starter?"

"Sure!" John smiled. "After this week, we're going to need a little rest and relaxation.

As John sat down, he opened his briefcase and a few things tumbled out. John looked down at the briefcase in disbelief. He looked at the door through which Anson had just made good his escape, then back down at his briefcase and shrugged his shoulders.

Quickly checking the case for all of its contents, he breathed a sigh of relief as he clicked it back together and set it on the floor. The look on his face seemed to say that he no longer suspected Anson of taking any belongings and was clearly disgusted with himself for putting his case hastily on the desk upside down.

19 The Con

Thursday – August 2, 1990 – Northrup

Mike O'Rourke paced in his office, carefully phrasing his words and rehearsing his body language. Mike wasn't very good at sleuth work and needed much practice to pull this acting job off, or so he thought.

Miss Van Briggle buzzed to let Mike know of his guest's anticipated arrival.

"Mr. Smithe to see you, sir," she purred.

"Good. Send him in, won't you, Miss Van Briggle?" he answered.

John was rarely summoned to the Director of Security and Internal Affairs' office, but when the occasion arose, he knew that something big was up. His heart beat quickened at the thought, that this might be the time that they caught him.

The feeling paralleled the same feeling one got when, in school, over the intercom, the school secretary announced that a certain child, namely you, be sent to talk to the Principal about something. No matter how good you had been, if you had to go to see the Principal, it must have been something pretty bad that you did. John was feeling those butterflies now.

"Mr. O'Rourke. Glad to see you. How may I be of service?" John asked as one of his moist palms clasped and held that of Mike O'Rourke's.

"Mike. Please call me Mike, John. Do you remember the deal we cut last October that had everything falling apart left and right before the deadline? I needed your help and you really pulled it off for us."

"I could use your expertise again, John," he sighed, "If you think you're up to it, I'll clear you for the Top Secret files in Contracts and Negotiations. You'll probably need to go over some of them to get all the wording just right."

"Well, sure Mike. But what's it all about? With so many new assistants up there, the load has been pretty well distributed. I had no idea that we were behind on anything," he seemed puzzled.

"And frankly, you wouldn't have. This one has been under wraps. We've been working on a cloaking device that would shield the B-2 from radar and heat detection. It would make it virtually undetectable to our adversaries. It's been up to the minute, around the clock, dedicated personnel working, trying to beat the deadline. This Friday, it has to be Federal Expressed to the Pentagon. Mike, we haven't even begun to put the final plans into writing. For a major contract like this, we really need someone who has worked a big Government project. All the others are rookies. I can't let someone cut their first teeth on something this important. What do you say? Will you take it upon yourself?"

"Well," John paused, "Will I have to work late? I have so many other projects that I'm presently working on...," he began.

"Absolutely not. You can work in the Top Secret File Room on this alone. We'll give your present case load to one of the other workers. Is there anyone in particular who you'd like to see take those items? I know, when you give birth to it, you'd probably like to see that it's raised by someone who's work you admire, eh?" he smiled.

"Well, I do get attached to my work. Emily Jasper has been very diligent in her efforts. I think I would feel comfortable handing her my present work," he started.

"About working late, with your experience and deleting your present load, I feel confident that you could accomplish this under normal working hours. When can you take a look at it?" Mike baited the hook.

"Right now. Just let me talk to Emily and I'll move my tools and things into the file room," John said.

"Very good. You do that. I'll have Dr. Brennery bring it to your personally. Thank you John. I knew I could count on you. Here, you'll need this. Of course, it won't get you any place other than the TS File Quarters, but that will be sufficient," Mike smiled, handing John his specialized orange TS badge.

After briefing Emily on his present files, John moved his items that were necessary for his job and his chair into the file room. An extra word processor was there already. It was secretly linked with Mike O'Rourke's processor so that he could monitor anything that was going on in the file room. John looked around the room.

There were three cameras that panned in all directions watching and waiting for treasonable characters to enter the chamber. Slowly John sat down and began his work, highly aware that every motion was being recorded.

John knew he had to work on the data as quickly as possible. He glanced over the plans and everything seemed to be in order. He mind was geared more for his line of work than for conceptional analyses of advanced technological discoveries. Perhaps that is why the exact details of this particular discovery were so important to him. This was what he had been waiting for. He had to get this right.

How would the nose of the craft remain cloaked if the velocity of the craft forces the cloud like fluid towards the center? That would leave the mid to rear of the plane exposed? That didn't sound like it would work, even to a novice in this area as he was. *Oh, well, it must work great or they wouldn't feel like they had a chance at the bid.*

On his lunch hour, Andie met Anson outside of the gate and they went to pick up their marriage license. With their blood work and physicals out of the way, they were excited to be starting a new phase of their lives.

20 Goal!

Friday afternoon came much too quickly. Anson only wished that he could contain his enthusiasm for the kill. He planned to speak to John on the way home about their golf game the next day. He decided he would carefully choose his words. He already knew that if everything went according to plan, there would be no golf game.

Andie had her own way of coping with the strain of the day. The tension she felt as she readied herself for the evening was mounting. Several times, she went into the surveillance room to check over the items that were so necessary in trapping her traitor.

She ran her hands over the cold steel as she cleaned her gun. She knew it well, as if it were her best friend. Every detail of the night's plan ran through her mind. There was something missing though; something she had to do. She slipped a tiny object into her pocket and went down to the hall closet.

Reaching into the closet, she withdrew a soccer ball and went out into the yard. There, sitting on the curb was a familiar face whose countenance glowed at the sight of Andie. Little Faith bounded over the grass to meet her friend.

"Would you like to play street soccer, Faith?" she asked.

"Would I? Sure I would!" she said gleefully.

"Alright then, there is my goal, by that brown car. Your goal will be by this Oak tree, got it?" she asked.

"Sure. Fire away.," Faith challenged.

"After several minutes of play, Andie strategically guided the ball right under the brown car parked by the curb in front of Faith's home. Faith rushed over to see if she would pry it out. Naturally, Andie made her move, calmly and swiftly bending down and placing the honing device under the bumper as she crawled under the car to retrieve the ball.

"Got it!" she smiled.

"I guess that was out of bounds, huh?" Faith asked innocently.

"It sure was, Faith. It sure was – that means you get a point!" she said tapping the car as she turned. Suddenly her spirit soared as if she had truly scored a goal.

Well maybe I never got the chance to bug the whole house, but at least I got the bugger's car!

Anson followed John to the elevator. He had seen John go to the Janitor's restroom today, so without hesitation, he knew that the blueprints had been photographed and the plan was still a go.

John set his briefcase down and adjusted his tie. Anson made his move. He set his identical case down inside of John's closest to John's knee, and did the same thing with his tie. Then suddenly, Anson hit his head with the palm of his hand.

"Darn! Wait here John. I've left something in the lab. I'll be right back," he said, lifting the case closest to his leg.

John didn't look down at the case until Anson was already in the airlock sealing himself within the confines of the lab. Panicking, John ran to the airlock glass and banged on the door. His attempts to get Anson's attention through the 12" tempered glass and over the noise of the shaker grates and sanitation blowers were in vain. Anson was facing away from him and silently knew what John was doing but paid no attention. He was safe so far.

Anson still could no longer hear what was going on outside as he stepped out of the airlock. Knowing shortly would be around the corner, he breathed a sigh of relief. Anson knew better than to look over his shoulder. The plan counted on the fact that he would not be able to see John. Joan Brennery met him at her office and they quickly frisked the outside of the case for the adhesive dot. Just when they were ready to panic, Anson found the familiar sticky dot. Reaching deep within his pocket, he found the duplicate adhesive micro dot and switched the two.

"I know that I gave him the phony bill of goods, but I don't want anyone to know just how close that plan IS! Thanks for switching it," Joan smiled.

"If this goes well, we won't be meeting like this anymore," Anson smiled.

"Too bad, too. Just when I was getting to like you Deputy Dawg. Just too bad that you're married too," she shook her head sadly.

"Not too bad. Kind' nice, actually," Anson winked, knowing that he would soon be a married man.

"Here, don't forget this. This is what you came for," she handed him some blank papers in an envelope with his name on the outside.

"Yeah, thanks Doc. Until we meet again," he saluted with the papers and was off running toward the airlock.

As Anson rounded the corner, he saw a very pale John with his body plastered against the glass trying to make some sort of contact with the inner world. Anson placed a well-rehearsed, puzzled look across his brow. "What?" he mouthed.

As he made it through the airlock, John reached for the case.

"You've got my brief case, Anson!" he snapped.

"Really, are you sure? I didn't open it. I just forgot to get this," he said waving the envelope.

John snapped the case away from him and twirled for the elevator. Nerves were at a snapping point already, and Anson tried to calm the waters.

"Hey, John. It was an honest mistake. Lighten up, will you'?" he asked.

"Yeah. I'm sorry. It's just all the pressure O'Rourke has me under the past two days. I never thought I would make the deadline. I'm sorry, really I am," he said.

"No matter. We'll relax when we get on the links tomorrow, huh? Nothing like taking your aggressions out on that little white ball, eh?" Anson gave him the elbow as they reached the bottom floor and moved out into the twilight of the evening.

When Anson arrived home, the others had already gotten there. They brought pizza and were watching videos of the Smithe home. They were discussing the relationship between Ivana and John. It was the general consensus that there might be more than just an accomplice, but felt it was better not to speculate.

With the blinds shut, the living room almost looked like the central meeting place for a group of terrorists. Everyone were dressed in black to help shield them through the night. Of course, their black jackets sported the letters FBI on the back in a reflective material kept them from looking like the bad guys. Should gunfire break out, this would make it easier to tell the good guys from the bad.

Kneeling down to load his M16 rifle, Jack spoke quietly to Anson.

"Listen, buddy. I already know where the rendezvous is going to be," he said.

"How could you? What intelligence have your guys gathered?" Anson asked.

"Remember the night of your party? You left out some minor details. What if something goes wrong and we can't tail her. Wouldn't it be prudent to have an idea where she was headed?" Jack smiled.

"Well, yes, but I thought we covered all of that. Andie bugged her car today. She told me she did," Anson insisted.

"Well I had Cappy follow her last Friday night and guess where she went?" Jack asked.

"You've got me. Alright, feeling like I'm a failure on my first job," Anson pouted.

"Hey! Don't be so down on yourself. You've done great, this being your first assignment and all. You just needed a little help with the details. De—tails will always get the little devils in the end you know?" he cracked himself up with his little joke.

"Okay. Great. Now where will she be going?" Anson Asked.

"Malibu beach. Well not quite. She met a whole raft full of guys there, gave them the information and they took off. Russians, they were. Cappy could tell by the dialect, but he doesn't know the language well enough to know what they were discussing," Jack Said.

"A raft full of Russian sailors just sailed up onto the beach, took spy stuff and then sailed off into the night?" Anson asked as his mouth dropped.

"Yeah. It's that simple, and I'll bet you that it's going down the same way tonight too. Now, Headquarters seems to think you have a friend at Point Magu in charge of Sea Traffic Controllers. Could you get him to could check something out for me?" asked Jack.

"Sure, but it can't be a trawler. They'd spot it miles away from here. It's got to be a sub. Good grief. A Russian attack submersible aimed at Point Magu as ransom. Would they be so bold?" Anson asked.

"Maybe. You know they are just training ex-flight jockeys to push those buttons and watch the screens. One probably is coming and going right under their noses and they don't even know what they are looking for," Jack offered.

"No Ray would. Trust me. If the Ax-man is on duty, no one is sleeping at the commands," Anson said.

"Okay, let's not panic. You get Point Magu on the phone and I'll alert the others," said Jack.

"Alert us to what?" asked Andie.

"Sit down, Andie. You're not going to believe this. Jack, I'll make the call," said Anson.

21 Subversive Vessel

As the Belle Starr made her way up the coastal route once more, as she did every Friday, the Boatswain's mate made his notations.

"Okay, Captain, here we go again. We've got somewhat appears to be wrong with the flipping' screen again. It's always right around these waters. Did you happen to check with any other Captains when we put into Port?" he asked.

"As a matter of fact, I did, but the answers were so varied in miles. Some that were Southbound experienced oceanographic disturbances in the ocean floor either hours before or after our encounters," he said.

"Sir, it's almost as if we have the Loch Ness Monster drifting under our bow, isn't it?" he said.

"No, it would have to be metal to get the ping reaction that we are getting. A metal Nessie, eh, Boatswain?" the Captain said, then paused for a moment.

"Boatswain, where exactly did you say we first encountered this?" the Captain asked.

"Well, it was around 3 miles off Long Beach and it stopped somewhere below the Ventura area – maybe Malibu?" he said.

Looking on the map, the Captain tried to remember where each Captain had encountered the phenomena. It seemed to be a constant flow of traffic along the Coastal route from the tip of Alaska down to the Mexican Border.

Whatever it is, it's catching rides under non-suspecting vessels. It seems to know which ones aren't Naval. They would pick it up in a hurry, wouldn't they? Why? Should I report it to the Naval Authorities? No. It's probably some of their subs having evasive tactical maneuvers – war games, that's all. Or should I?

"You know Boatswain; you may be onto something there. I'm going to report it to the Point Mugu Sea Controller. They'll probably think that I'm crazy, but I just can't take the chance that it's an enemy subversive vessel," said the Captain.

Point Mugu Naval Air Station - 23:00 hours – Sea Controller Commander's Office

Ensign Parker stared at the screen. There it was again. He had studied each blip until his eyes ached and watered begging for rest. It was definitely a submarine by his markings, but it couldn't be a Russian. He would have tracked it in on sonar hours ago, no, days ago. They would have easily stopped it in Alaska at the twelve-mile mark. Then could something be wrong with the screen? The Computer program wouldn't have a glitch, would it? He felt odd about consulting with the Commander. He was on the phone with an old buddy from Miramar Naval Air

Station near San Diego where he was active at Top Gun. He would just have to wait until he got off the phone.

Ray couldn't believe his ears. He thought Anson Wellings had dropped off the face of the earth and now to hear his voice after these past few years did him proud to hear his "hero" student was still alive.

"You were one of my best pilots there at Top Gun, Anson. Why didn't you take me up on the offer to stay there and help me teach? You would have been a great asset to the program," Ray wanted to know.

"I don't know, Ray, but I really like doing what I am doing now," said Anson.

"Yeah, FBI. They're lucky to have you, guy. It's a long way from the fast moving birds thought. What can I do for you? I'll tell you right now, I can't let you have a carrier for the weekend. I'd never be able to push that paper work through," he laughed.

"Well, it's a little easier than that. You might think it's a crazy hunch thought. We think there might be a Russian Submarine lurking off the coast right next to you, Ray. Any possible chance that you could already be on top of that case?" Anson almost waited for Ax-man to laugh in his face.

"This is a joke, right Wellings? You really think we'd let one just wash up on shore?" he laughed.

"Well, like I said, it was just a hunch. We're trying to break up a spy ring and Russians are the main operatives that we are trying to defeat and capture. We're going to be following a lead heading out to the coast probably within an hour or two. If we're right, it would be nice to have a little muscle behind us from your end," Anson said.

"Well, give me your number and I'll get right back to you after I check out some data," said Ray.

"Ray, if this is for real, Washington wants us to keep it real low profile. We are to assist them and escort them out of our waters then notify President Yeltsin of our assistance. President Bush is in the loop.

"A spy ship? Let it go? Just like that? What are they thinking anyway?" he chuckled.

"None the less, minimal resistance and a show of good will. I'm sure you remember what will happen to them all just for the embarrassment of getting caught." He didn't have to remind Ray. He had seen it before. These sailors would rather be shot than return home under humiliation of getting caught by an Amerikanski. They faced, torture, exile to Siberia or death and of course, death to his family members first. He said it before.

"Alright, just for fun, let me ask one of the guys. Hey, any of you throttle monkeys seen any possible Russian fish swimming in our depths?" Ray said just loud enough for Anson to hear him snickering on the other end of the line.

"Sir," Ensign Parker began, "as a matter of fact, I was going to speak to you briefly about that. I had a hunch a while back but I was sure that it was wrong. I mean, I never tracked it. It just appeared," he said meekly.

"Ray's jaw dropped and his cigar dropped to his lap. As he fumbled for the right end, he spoke brusquely to Anson, "Call you back, Lieutenant Wellings. If you're right, I'll meet you for a drink at the Officer's club when this is all over, eh?" he tried to sound calm.

Not waiting for a reply, he slammed the phone down and arose with a vengeance. Ray Axman was not a man to be made a fool of, especially by a rookie. How could they have missed something so obvious? Ray bellowed orders left and right as he made his way around Central Command. Peering into the screen, he tapped the blip with the butt of his cigar.

"There she is, a sitting duck. I've got to call Washington on this one, boys. We're either going to be famous for finding her or court martialed for letting her have this kind of access so close to a Naval Air Station. Start saying your prayers boys, we're going to need them," he said turning towards the phone.

"Sir," said a voice, "I just got the strangest call from the Captain of an Oil Tanker, The Belle Starr. He explained that he and other Captains have been tracking something that has been cruising at their speed directly under their bows. At first they thought it was just a rift in the Continental shelf from El Nino. This guy has pin pointed several incidences from the Tip of Alaska to the Mexican Border. Sir? Sir, what do you think? Is this a practical joke?" repeated one of the seamen.

"Practical joke? I want you to deploy a chopper a go out and make a visit. Give them these coordinates and make sure they are fully armed. Do nothing, however. Return recon report directly to me."

As the Commander placed the call to Anson's dwelling the two vehicles pulled away from the driveway in search of the brown car which had turned onto Kanan Road. She was on her way to Malibu Beach. Receiving no answer, his next call was to the Oval Office.

22 The Cavalry

When Anson, Andie and the rest reached the beach, they turned off their lights and pulled off the road. They got out, gear intact, and crouched next to the bumper.

"Are we it? Where's the Cavalry, Gibbens?" said Andie.

"They're here somewhere. Cappy brought them. They're hiding out down there on the beach. They live for this stuff, you know that!" he smirked.

"I knew that," Anson lied.

Andie elbowed Anson in a half joking way as she looked across the highway. Anson looked up to see a signal from a ship being sent ship to shore. Ivana had a signal light also and was using it in return.

"What's she saying, Andie?" asked Bess.

"I can't tell what she's saying, her back is to me, but they are sending in Russian, WAIT – 10 – MINUTES – HELP COMING," she said.

*　　　*　　　*　　　*　　　*　　　*　　　*

"This is Apache AH64, calling Control. Come in Control."

"Control to Apache AH64 – over."

"Control Be advised stroll in the park found the missing child. Apache AH64 over."

"Apache AH64 confirm target sighted – Control over."

"Control you have a Vic's Vaporub 2 in your backyard. – Apache AH64 over."

"Apache AH64 – repeat and confirm Vaporub2 – Control over."

"Control – Sir, you're not going to believe this. – Apache AH64 over"

"Apache AH64 – try me, son – Control over."

"Control – Sir she looks dead in the water well inbound of 12 miles. Should I offer assistance? She appears to be signaling the shore; radio could be out – Apache AH64 – over."

"Apache AH64 – stand by and go whisper– Control over."

"Control – whisper and ready."

Ray turned to his crew who were listening with eyes wide open. "You heard correctly. That's a Victor Class 2 Soviet Nuclear Submarine, Gentlemen. How and why she roamed 9 miles inside International waters, and pointed right at our Naval Air Station, we will find out, but for now, we need to call this to DC. Now everybody, one is enough, but I would appreciate it if you would watch your screens for anymore, clear?"

A combined audible, "Aye sir!" – bellowed from the room.

"Apache AH64," the Ax-man started, "Good work son, return to base, offer no assistance at this time, stay in whisper for 5 clicks, repeat, no assistance at this time – Control over and out," Ray spoke slowly and deliberately as his mind swiftly kicked into gear.

"Apache AH64 – You're the boss Commander - returning to base – over and out" said the pilot as he banked right and began his return in whisper mode.

"One more thing, Pilot. I want you to check on something...," he said as his voice lowered and gave the next set of commands in a hushed whisper.

"Alright, boys and girls, here's the plan. We need to deploy a few cruisers and a couple of subs of our own. We'll form our own little blockade of assistance, as the good Pilot suggested. They have two choices, as I see it. They'll either play sick, or make a run for it. We'll be ready before we offer the Doctors to surgically remove their appendix. Let's get this thing going. Notify Washington of what I am up against. I want to keep a direct line open to President Bush on this one. Notify the Captains of the USS California and the USS Pasadena to sound general quarters

- both are on patrol in the Monterey and Santa Barbara Areas, let's get them down here," said Ray.

"Do you think they are heavily armed, sir?" asked one of the men.

"Armed, dangerous and close enough to plant a very noisy present on the Former President Reagan's Ranch, but we're going to fix all that, son."

"They wouldn't dare upset Glasnost, would they sir?" asked a nervous young woman.

"There are lots of Political Officers who don't believe in Glasnost, heck they don't even like Yeltsin. They'd do anything to make him look bad. Now, our President wants us to keep a low profile on this and set the fish free for whatever reason. Trust me, when Boris gets hold of them, they'll be pulling frozen undies off the lines in Siberia for a long while, if they are lucky," said Ray.

*   *   *   *   *   *   *   *   *   *   *   *
*

The long sleek lines of the B-414 Daniil Moskovskiy glistened in the moonlight with engines were silent yet sailors scattered to alert their Captain of the chopper overhead. That the Americans had discovered their hiding place was a disgrace!

"Capitansky! They know we're here. What shall we do," asked the worried man.

"It was only a matter of time," the Capitan answered in his native tongue.

"You should have stayed submerged," nagged the Political Officer aboard the ship.

"I am and will always be the Capitan of this boat. You are here merely to protect Mother Russia against defecting swine. Do not tell me what to do, Comrade Smolinsky," he bellowed.

"What then will you do?" he wanted to know.

"Disable the radio and let some oil leak out into this bay. We will plead innocent of any wrong doings. Signal the away team to get back here. I do not want to be found with evidence against us," said the wise Capitan.

"Yes, Capitansky," replied the dutiful Officer as he relayed the message to the rest of the crew.

23 Oil Slick?

"Patch me through to Sea Command at Magu, please Inez," said Anson. Inez got on the radio and made the vital connection.

"Commander Waxman, please. It's a matter of National Security. Tell him it's Lieutenant Wellings, he'll understand," she said.

The wait was brief before Ray exploded onto the set. "Anson, I tried to reach you. Boy when you guys party, you invite all the wrong guests, don't you?" he said.

"Ray, it's going down. They made the switch. Can I count on you for back up?" he asked.

"They're on their way, ETA is 7 minutes. What is the away team doing right now?" he asked.

"Just standing there on the beach talking. Andie said that the raft is being recalled," he said.

"Who's Andie?" asked Ray

"She's...," he paused, "my partner." Had he really said that? Was he finally admitting that she was a good partner, that he could work with a female?

"Alright, I'm aboard an LST. We are on an intercept course with the sub right now," Anson could barely hear Ray over the powerful engines.

"I'll pick you up for a debriefing when I have the situation stabilized," said Ray. He couldn't see Anson nod and click off.

One at a time, each agent serpentined their way across the busy highway and dove into the sandy shoal. Anson was the last to go across. Anson came up sputtering sand but it was drowned out by the deafening waves.

All guns were trained on the frogmen and Ivana. Suddenly from the hidden bunkers of sand, one lone man rose and stood. Anson and Andie started counting heads and could not make out who this was. Demanding recognition, he said, "FREEZE, FBI!" Who was this guy? This was not in the plans.

He alone could see that Ivana was drawing her weapon as she began to turn towards him. This was enough for him to squeeze off a shot, but he missed. Ivana, a trained markswoman in her own right, aimed straight for his heart. Dodging the bullet, it missed his heart by milliseconds, taking a direct hit to the shoulder.

It was time for the others to let their presence be known. Andie squeezed off a round in the moonlight and Ivana's gun flew away from her grip and was cast into the sand. "FREEZE! FBI! Anyone who moves will be shot on sight. Throw down your weapons," she said in perfect Russian.

The men shot glances at each other. Holding their hands high in the air, they wondered if they would be searched for contraband. Could the Americans possibly know that we already have the information in our possession that we need? How could they be so stupid as to let us go? They decided to play along with the unintelligent bourgeois capitalists.

"Please, madam," one spoke slowly and distinctly in broken English. "There was no radio and we had not a way to communicate with your Government. And it is possible that our ship is still losing oil, even as we speak, if our crewmen have not already fixed the leak," this Senior officer clearly knew plan B; the one to use in case of capture.

"Yes, Lady Capitansky, we were desperate. Is it possible for your Government to help us?" another asked.

"Of course. We will do anything to preserve the spirit of Glasnost and Perestroika. However, I was unaware that you had a female Political Officer aboard. I didn't see her get off your raft. It seems rather daring, even for a Socially reformed progressive Country such as yours," Andie mused.

The Senior Officer played right into her hand. He thought he was so smart, and Andie was clearly having fun with the mind games that she was imposing. The rest of her team were not fluent in Russian, so they just acted the part of informed team members and played along with whatever she was saying.

"Yes, Lady Capitansky. These are changing times; I believe you refer to them as "the 90's, yes? It is difficult to have such a beautiful Political Officer aboard, but it is an exercise in discipline, you understand," he lied.

"I understand. You may all get into your raft. I am sure that you must realize that we have been aware of your presence for quite some time. We merely were waiting for you to contact us for assistance. We knew that you had no intention of trying to destroy our Country, naturally," she could lie too.

"Your submarine is surrounded by our finest capitalist nuclear submarines and missile cruisers, Comrade. Naturally, a rescue crew has arrived at your vessel to assist your Capitansky. By the time you arrive, they should be ready to tow your boat to the International waters. We have informed your General Secretary Yeltsin of the assistance. Should you need further assistance, he has arranged for a large fishing trawler from your country to help you get back home safely," she smiled.

As they got into the raft, Ivana said nothing. She looked back on the beach where the suitcase lay filled with American money. Money that was meant for the wife of her prisoner. Jenny Smithe, a former socialite, had been reduced to a captive in her own home. Ivana used Jenny to get to John. She got her hooked on intravenous drugs and the only reason John was blackmailed into helping was to get the money to get treatment for his wife once this nightmare was over.

Sadly, when the backup team arrived at John Smithe's home, they found him badly beaten and tied up, Faith was locked in a closet, Jenny was in a coma and no money was on the premises. They knew Ivana had double crossed him. She had given Jenny an almost lethal dose and did not think that John would survive.

Her intention was to leave no witnesses. She cared very little about leaving Faith an orphan. Luckily before she was locked in the closet, little Faith had grabbed the cordless phone off the nightstand next to her mother. Ivana did not see this, nor had she a clue that Faith had called 911 and rescued her parents in the nick of time.

Now Ivana stared at the woman who spoke Russian and who had all her money. She was angry but she dared not try to retrieve it. Instead, in a magnanimous gesture, she called to the Agents.

In broken English, she said, "Of course, in the suitcase, you will find a present for your President for assisting our Government," she called through the pounding waves.

"I'll bet," murmured Jack.

"Nice cover," Andie laughed.

"What in the world did she mean by that?" asked Bess.

"Cover up, my dear, covering her tail," said Harry.

"I'd still like to blast them. No one could blame me you know. It would feel good...," Inez tried to convince herself of the possibility.

"Now, now, Ms. Caruso," calmed Anson as he waved and smiled in the darkness. "It's true. She thinks she has gotten away with quite a coup, but when she delivers the picture on the dot, she'll get blasted by her Political Officer for sure, only he will be KGB, and she may be shot for treason. So you see, no matter what we could do, by going home in shame, she sealed their fate."

"Really? What did you put on that dot?" Inez wanted to know.

Anson only laughed as he helped Cappy to his feet.

"So you're Cappy, eh? I've wondered when I was going to meet you? Where are all these other agents who were going to meet us there?" Anson wanted to know, not knowing about Faith alerting 911 and the FBI intercepting the call, and coming to her rescue.

"A minor communication problem, sir," Cappy sheepishly grinned. "I forgot to call them."

"You _what_?" Harry stomped through the sand and grabbed the injured man's collar. "We could have all been blown away out here? How could you be so impetuous as to think you could ever do this along?" he demanded.

"Hero. The first rule is don't be a hero and get others in jeopardy."

"I don't know, sir. I just saw her with the gun and I knew that I had to act," said Cappy.

"And right you did. However, if it hadn't been for my partner, shooting the Red's number one agent's gun from her hand, we'd probably all be dead, right now. Here Andie, you deserve this," said Anson, picking up the sandy Russian luger and brushing it off.

"Why Anson, I'm touched," she said.

"Accept it as a wedding present, won't you? Well, it's really evidence, but you can hold onto it for now. I'll try to get the authorities to release it," he said.

"Wedding present? Are you getting married, Andie? To whom?" asked Bess.

"To the best partner a girl could have, Bess," she smiled.

"Why Harry! Right under our noses. How could this have happened?" Bess asked.

"I'll tell you how, Bess. Just turn back the clock, my dear, just turn back the clock," he said as he grabbed her hand and walked towards the car.

"Come on, Inspector Caruso. Let's get Cappy to the Hospital. Give me a hand, will you?" Harry said as he helped Cappy towards the cars.

*   *   *   *   *   *   *

The Capitansky of the Daniil Moskovskiy sat in his cabin, waiting for word of the Americans to arrive. Soon, it was imminent that his presence was requested up top and he knew he was trapped but mustered the courage to play it cool.

"I thank you Commander, for your assistance," he practically choked on the words in broken English. He hated admitting defeat.

"What can we do to help? It appears you have an oil leak," he spoke as his nostrils flared at the pungent smelling pollution fouling his precious ocean.

"Yes, we have had it for several days, but we were unable to fix it," he lied. "We drifted here to avoid using our engines. Our crew has just found the leak and repaired it. If you will kindly lend us some oil, and escort us into International Waters, we will be on our way," The Capitansky squirmed under duress.

Ray knew that he was, of course, lying. Before returning back to base, he had also ordered the Apache AH64 pilot to track back any slicks back from International Waters. As far as the attack helicopter pilot could tell, with his floodlight, the oil slick surrounded only the Russian vessel, but had not been trailed to the coastline from International Waters. The leak was a deliberate dump to avoid persecution and they both knew it, but what could he do. The Ax-Man had his orders.

"And your radio, Capitansky? Did it suddenly start working as well? Perhaps you would allow a few of my men to board your ship and repair it for you. Naturally, in the spirit of Glasnost...," Ray said with a smirk on his face.

"That won't be necessary, Commander. I would imagine that you have already informed our Government of our problem. I am sure that someone will meet us, who will have Russian radio components," he said with a sneer.

"Naturally, Capitansky," Ray spoke mockingly, "Ah, I see that your landing party has arrived. We will begin. Are your engines functional at this time, or would you like us to tow you?" he teased.

"Commander, let us disperse with the games. I am sure that you know they have always been fully functional," the Capitansky snapped, suddenly sick of this charade of mocked politeness. His glance even in the moonlight, said that he wished to tell the Commander exactly how he felt. He wanted to tell him that if he wanted to, his Victor Class 2 Soviet Nuclear Submarine could have blown most of California to bits, he bragged silently. But what could he do? Admit to a major incident? Admit to spying? He had to play along, but how he despised being the mouse in this game of wills.

As the landing party was helped aboard, the Capitansky's eyebrows raised to see the lovely young woman escorting the four men. He was puzzled. He knew who she was and he knew that she had been caught red handed and he hated her for putting him and his crew in peril.

"Nyet. What are YOU doing here?" he hissed.

She quickly turned her back to the Americans and hissed, "Quiet! They think that I am your Political Officer, serving as liaison in requesting aid. Just play along," she spat back, trying to smile under the noise of the engines.

"That will be the day, when the Motherland puts a woman in charge of a vessel like this. Then I WILL defect!" he whispered.

The real Political Officer was confused and his eyebrows rose sharply when he heard the word defect.

"The captain shook his finger at her and said, "You have killed us all. I can't take any more part in such a capitalist plot against Russia. No females on my boat," he whispered hoarsely.

"You will do it or you will be charged with spying," she paused. "Now, whether you look like a fool or not, get us out of here and quickly. I've got what I came for and they have no knowledge of this," she said through her teeth as she waved to the American Commander. Commander Waxman's shadow against the spotlight of the LST shining on the sub was an impressive image.

Standing on his boat directly amidships, Ray shot a hushed whisper to his interpreter. "What's she talking to him about?" asked Ray.

"I'm not sure, sir. It's too far to hear them," said his interpreter.

"Well, what the heck is the hold up. You are not doing me much good, are you?" He forced a smile from the side of his mouth without the cigar.

"Commander, again, we thank you. We are ready to get under way. Dos vedanya!" he saluted Ray.

"Good-bye Captainsky. Let us hope we never have to meet under combat, shall we?" Ray waited for the interpreter to translate and then gave the Russian Captain a final salute.

With a reticent return salute out of respect and a final nod of his head, the Russian Captain disappeared through the hatch.

24 Fully Cloaked

Anson and Andie held hands as they sat on the beach waiting for Ray to pick them up in the Landing transport. The LST had the capability to come right up to the beach and drop its front hull for the Sailors to disembark. It was finally over. They could get on with their lives and become man and wife. They could relish their new found religion with full intensity. Both had a drive within their hearts to learn so much. It was almost as if they felt that they had been cheated all those years of learning in Primary and Young Women's and Young Men's Organizations.

All those years that people born under the Covenant within the walls of the Church take for granted. It seemed such a shame to them, that young people could take such precious knowledge for granted. The spark of enthusiasm that dwelled within the hearts of all converts lit the Spirit of Fire that burned in their bosoms.

"Anson, where will we live?" she asked.

Anson said nothing and stared into the waves.

"Anson, do you remember what they said at the beginning? That we could have any transfer that we wanted, with full pay and an honor bonus. Where will we go, Anson?" she didn't want to make the decision alone.

"How do you feel about staying here? I mean, it's so beautiful and after all, we've made friends in the Ward.

After all, the Bishop there is going to marry us. I'd really like him and his family to go with us to the Temple next year, wouldn't you?" he asked.

"Oh yes, Anson, could we?" she asked.

"Well, actually I'd have to check with my new partner. It couldn't be my decision alone," he said.

Andie stared at the waves in wide eyed horror. The black of the night saved her from her shock on her face being seen. That was right. He wanted the whole nine yards. She would have to give up her career, her dreams, aspirations to help her country. He would get a new partner. All that she had worked for would now have to fit neatly into a little compromised package.

"Of course. When the Director reassigns you...," she began unselfishly.

"No. I mean, you. You're the best partner that a guy could ask for. Do you think we could work together for a little while longer, even as husband and wife? We work so well together. We could, I think, keep going until you choose, I mean, we choose...no, until Heavenly Father chooses for us to conceive a child.," he said as he played with the sand.

A light in the distance showed a landing craft approaching the shore. Andie knew that it would be many hours of debriefing before they would have a chance to talk again.

She threw her arms around his neck and kissed his cheek. Knocking him over playfully in the sand, he lay on his back smiling up into her eyes.

"See, you did it again. You took me down," he laughed.

"We were good, weren't we Wellings?" she asked.

"I think the Director would have been proud, don't you?" he smiled as he helped her to her feet and walked toward the boat which was rocking gently on the shore, to greet Commander Ray Waxman.

"Wait, Anson. You've got to tell me. What was on the dot that you let her take back to her country?" Andie asked.

"I don't think you want to know. You might not marry me if you find out what kind of twisted humor I have," said Anson.

"Oh yeah? Try me. You've got to tell me right now!" she pouted.

"Alright, come here," he held her close and whispered what he had photographed into her ear.

"Andie burst out laughing and said, "Okay! I'll marry you. That was pretty good!"

August 4, - - Aboard the Daniil Moskovskiy Soviet Victor 2 Nuclear Submarine – North West Pacific Ocean – 11:00 AM

Ivana worked furiously to get the film into the computer. From there, the computer merely enhanced and enlarged the dot until the image was large enough to print.

Ivana's English was pretty good, but it took her a few seconds to realize that she had been HAD. *The subtlety of English humor is so unintelligent,* she thought as she slumped into a chair outside the door.

The Capitansky happened to come down the hall towards the wardroom as her head fell into her lap.

"Comrade, tell me that you did not risk the lives of all the crew members for nothing. You did get the information on the cloaking device, did you not?"

"Capitansky, look for yourself. You are looking at a dead woman. You are looking at a woman who will spend the rest of her life farming icicles in Siberia. I will probably be taking you and your crew with me, I am much afraid," she said.

The Capitansky ducked into the dark room to have a look for himself. There, clearly on the screen of the computer was a toy model of a new B2 Bomber, suspended over the sink by fishing line. It was pointed downward towards the sink as if it were going to crash and go down the drain.

Written in perfectly formed computer lettering, were the words: "Your plan to copy our airship just went down the sink, my friend."

The Captain had to chuckle. *They knew all the time,* he thought. *Ah, it is all a game, is it not Ivana? We have lost this round only, but perhaps there will be others, Lieutenant. Wellings. Yes, we've known about you too...*

THE END

About The Author

Karen Meyer is the mother of 5 and step mother of 7. She and her husband Ted are avid Genealogists. She has written several novels, each having a variety on a spiritual theme and all are either mystery and intrigue or romance novels.

When asked why she chose to write novels with a moral theme, she answered, "It's not enough that people learn something valuable from a "feel good story". As the breakdown of the family unit has evolved in the past century, we have lost a lot of valuable teaching moments within the home. We need to transplant good family values back into the system by creating works that do not offend the mind with salty language and show consequences for good and evil. If a story can change or soften a heart into making choices to do more good in the world, then I've done my job as an author." ~ Karen S. Meyer

Made in the USA
Middletown, DE
03 May 2024

53821793R00106